Rolf Goerke's novel is gripping! Although this novel is fiction, Rolf captures many elements of the Idaho Backcountry that are very accurate today, and that could only be described by someone having experienced this unique culture from the inside. Rolf has this knowledge and perspective from being a long-term Wilderness Ranger for the US Forest Service in the same magical geography of the Frank Church River of No Return Wilderness that he describes. The messages delivered here are guttural, the story line riveting, and the setting brought to life with vivid and colorful descriptions that transcend time and place. It is not possible to spend time in Sheepeater Country and not imagine how the indigenous people lived, loved the land – and its creatures, related to each other, and ultimately felt about their own tragic removal by the US Army in 1879. Like Rolf, I too have walked the same trails and felt the same seasonal change and nuances that the Sheepeater Indians, or Tukudika, did for millennia. Rolf skillfully weaves into his characters the enlightenment brought by wilderness and the deep reflections of those *willing to imagine…*

-Jim Akenson, *7003 Days, 21 years in the Frank Church River of No Return Wilderness*

The Last Sheepeater

Rolf Goerke

Pocol Press
Clifton, VA

POCOL PRESS
Published in the United States of America
by Pocol Press
6023 Pocol Drive
Clifton, VA 20124
www.pocolpress.com

Publisher's Cataloguing-in-Publication
Names: Goerke, Rolf, 1938-, author.
Title: The Last sheepeater / Rolf Goerke.
Description: Clifton, VA: Pocol Press, 2018.
Identifiers: ISBN 978-1-929763-79-5 | LCCN 2018933896
Subjects: LCSH Tukuarika Indians--Fiction. | Indians of North America--Idaho--Fiction. | Idaho--Fiction. | Short stories, American. | BISAC
FICTION / Native American & Aboriginal | FICTION / Short Stories
(single author) |
Classification: LCC PS3607.O335 L37 2018 | DDC 813.6--dc23

Library of Congress Control Number: 2018933896

DEDICATION

For Margaret

TABLE OF CONTENTS

1. Those First Europeans 1

2. Wolf 6

3. Why Not? 13

4. Government Mule 20

5. Back to Eden 26

6. Bushmen of the Kalahari 31

7. All of Creation 38

8. The King 45

9. That We Too May Endure 54

10. Then Go To Her 61

11. Touch of Breeze 71

12. Medicine Peak Country 79

13. Besides Just Up More Mountains 86

14. Off to the Hunt 91

15. The Last Sheepeater 111

16. Into the Clouds 131

1. Those First Europeans

Shipwrecked on the other side of the ocean, off the coast of what is now Texas, those first Europeans, rubbing the salt water from their eyes, found themselves among a brown-skinned people who went about naked and in deerskins—the women more vibrantly alive and beautiful than any they had ever seen.

Four of the shipwrecked men survived by joining into the life of the people whose land it was.

For several glorious months those people lived mainly on the new, tender pads of prickly pear, as well as gorged on its juicy red fruits as plump as eggs. And when that ran out, they lived on roots, spiders, worms, lizards, snakes, and animal dung— and an occasional fish, or deer that had been run to exhaustion. And occasionally, for three or four days straight—they ate nothing.

Sometimes the bearded ones, as they came to be called, would join the people at night in the flickering torchlight, where lulled by strange, pounding rhythms, they all partook of a spineless cactus and its tea—that helped one enter the other, more real world from which all things emanate.

And that helped one to see—and to talk with God.

With time, the survivors no longer found the ground hard, especially sleeping as they usually did alongside a beautiful, young, brown-skinned woman—who in the darkness of night became even more vibrantly alive. More so than anything they had ever imagined.

And from that other world from which all things emanate, as well as from the unfathomable earth knowledge contained in those women, four Europeans—four Spanish conquistadors—received inklings that all about them, as well as deep within them, there lurked a Power that was much greater than all of Spain.

The shaman picked up a smooth round stone. Then handed it to the bearded, bony-ribbed, white man burnt almost as dark as himself, the two of them as naked as the day they were born.

The shaman said, "If I—who am no more than what you see before you—together with the Soul-Spirit lodged in this little stone—am able to restore the health of a brother—surely you who have come from the Heaven That Lies Beyond the Sunrise—must possess even greater magic."

"It has never occurred to me to try to cure anyone—I am by no means God."

"The Great Spirit can always use our help—you must at least try."

And the shaman sent word to bring the sick.

The bearded man knelt down. And as he stared at the smooth brown face, and into the beseeching eyes, he saw the harshness and strangeness of this vast wilderness he was captive of—saw his own loneliness and terror.

Nevertheless, tracing the sign of a cross, he began quietly reciting Pater Nosters and Ave Marias. Until suddenly a fiery wind taking hold inside him, he found himself alternately blowing up and down the body and praying fervently for every man's deliverance, and for his own—acting with such utter intent and conviction that it inspired the sick man, who already believed in the bearded man's magic and whose eyes turned wildly expectant, to believe even more.

And just like that the man jumped up cured—and smiling broadly, gave the bearded God all his food and possessions. And that day, others too were cured.

Soon people were converging from the four directions, bringing gifts of venison and deerskins and their love and faith.

The same bearded man, one day accompanying some of the people in the dead of winter on a far-ranging search for scant food, became separated from them.

And lost his way.

Pushed frantically through thorns that bloodied feet and body, trying to find his way back to them.

Toward nightfall, exhausted and trembling with the cold, the Lord leads him to a tall burning tree. And there, humble and thankful, he digs a shallow hole, that he lines with branches. He gathers sticks and dry grass, and some embers. And builds four fires, signifying a cross, around the hole. Finally he lies down in the hole, wrapping his naked, wild animal body in grass, and his just as naked soul in a prayer. And falls asleep.

The next day, wandering hungry and naked, carrying with him some embers and sticks for the next fire, he stops to watch helpless, as the final remnant of what was once Álvar Núñez Cabeza de Vaca, the Spaniard who washed ashore six years before—is snatched away from him by a swift-running fox.

Several nights later, asleep in another burrow, lit by a flaming cross, he is jerked awake by tears of joy and the knowledge that everything is exactly as it should be, a love bubbling and welling up in him that is boundless and annihilates all possibility of defeat, and of death too.

As did the mystery of God's love made manifest on the cross.

Nor did he think it odd when the next day, sensing himself guided as if by an invisible hand, he heard, wafting down from heaven, the song of a child. Nor, when following in the direction of that celestial song, he came upon several scattered, inhabited stick and bark huts.

Nor was he the least bit amazed, when—looking upon the disorbited eyes of a dead man with no pulse and whose hut his neighbors had already torn down—so much love came gushing out of his heart for the poor soul, that the dead man opened his eyes, and then, slowly, struggled to his feet.

Soon, throughout the land, the people spoke of little else.

The fox dances into a patch of moonlight, vibrantly alive, wildly beautiful, and her head suddenly turning, halts to contemplate the creature that is observing her. The tail swishes once, and a second time—the eyes locking onto, penetrating those of the other.

The fox speaks. "It seems you are no longer a Spaniard—yet those you live among can never be your people either—nor will you ever be able to turn yourself back into anything even halfway resembling say a deer or a fox—so what are you then?"

"I think—I think I may be someone who can love—these people and this land—and you a fox—and I also think that you and I may have—in some fashion—already known each other since before the earth began."

"Those having never known love—will oppose those who have with their whole being—and with every cruelty imaginable."

And she streaks off into the darkness.

The four bearded men begin a journey in the direction of the setting sun, hoping to eventually meet up with others of their kind.

The people from one place accompanying them to the next people.

Everywhere, the four Children of the Sun, as they came to be called, were greeted by hands that touched the bearded faces and then their own smooth ones, and by piles of food and goods. And always those who accompanied them, when it was time to return to where they had come from, wept.

Tribes that fought their neighbors became friends so that all could greet the visitors, give them everything they had— and to take part in the procession making its way toward the setting sun.

A procession that had by now turned into a pilgrimage of healing and celebration. That at times numbered as many as a thousand.

Leaving in its wake not only many persons healed—but also a land shimmering in peace.

Day after day of brush and tall grass flat land—here and there a river, a few low trees. Then days of sparsely-vegetated and almost waterless, yellow desert and mountains.

The multitude following the plunging sun.

A joining of two great rivers. A sprinkling of permanent, earthen houses alongside plots of corn, beans, and squash. Whose people coexisted and traded with nomads who hunted deer and buffalo and who dug up sotol and agave hearts that they roasted in dirt-covered pits.

Dazzlingly beautiful women, like splendid suns, the deep pools of their eyes promising eternity.

Gifts of turquoise gemstones from the north—along with rumors of jeweled cities.

The procession nevertheless maintaining its momentum—the rhythm and the miraculousness of the happening being unstoppable.

The Children of the Sun giving thanks to God, from whom all good things descend.

They wind up a rocky, broken escarpment, through oaks, then pines, some fatter than a man is tall. A tangle of abrupt canyons, rugged peaks, and sheer cliffs. Finally reach the sky. Then begin to wind back down among more canyons and peaks and cliffs.

And then one day, suddenly, dangling from around a neck—a Spanish-made buckle with a horseshoe nail attached to it. Along with stories of bearded men like themselves, who mounted on horses and brandishing lances had descended from who knows where, burning and destroying villages— and had led many away in chains. And stories about those who had managed to flee, abandoning homes and fields to hide in the mountains.

And so word spread of two races of bearded men: one which came from where the sun went down, and another that came from where

4

it rose. One came lavishly dressed and mounted on horses, and the other naked and on foot. One tortured and killed, and the other cured the sick. One took whatever caught its eye, and the other coveted nothing.

Those who had fled into the mountains came out of hiding to welcome the approaching miracle, bringing with them as gifts their uncontainable smiles and every last bit of food they had.

The four naked survivors smell the salt air of the coast.

Two days later they meet up with a Spanish slave-raiding party. And put back on the strange clothes of proper, civilized Christians.

A month later, in Mexico City, received in the splendid palace of Hernán Cortés, with a plate of turkey mole before him, and raising a crystal goblet of blood-red wine to his lips, the man who had once sought refuge in an animal-like burrow, and who had tasted and knew many things that even if they could be explained would never be understood—blinks several times.

And tries with all the might of his magic, and then tries again to make the jagged pieces, the shapes and colors and textures of this once so familiar and so solid and comfortable world in which he is again seated—glide, snap back into place.

But can only conjure up a vast sprawling wilderness, extending across an entire continent—and inhabited by bear, deer, antelope, and buffalo, and by mountain lions and wolves, and ducks and turkeys, and high-soaring eagles.

And inhabited too, everywhere, by generation after generation of brown-skinned men, women, and children.

That same night, he who had been twice visited by a fox, dreams of a fox more beautiful than the most beautiful woman—she lying on her side in a green meadow, and bleeding,

Bleeding and bleeding—and spilling over the land more rivers of blood than could possibly have come from a fox.

Or from even tens of thousands of foxes.

2. Wolf

Paul, sitting alongside Anne on a green metal bench in a small park that overlooks the Mississippi River, tries to ignore the roar of the traffic from the freeway below. Directly across the river from them, in Illinois, is the Cahokia World Heritage Site.

That hundreds of years before the first Europeans set foot on the continent, Cahokia was a flourishing urban center—the largest north of what is now southern Mexico—had from the very first intrigued Paul to no end.

But even more it had it intrigued him that its Monk's Mound, the largest man-made earth structure in North America, along with a hundred lesser mounds, served as a major astronomical and religious center.

Not long after he and Anne had moved here, to East St. Louis, he began to have strange dreams.

In the first dream, a brown Indian woman wearing nothing but a knee-length skirt and a small backpack, and with a live rattlesnake coiled on her head, and ears of corn tied to her ankles, handed him a decorated ceramic vessel—from which he drank. After which, she picking up her hoe, led him by the hand up to the flat square top of one of the earthen mounds.

Where he began to feel a strangeness throughout his body, as if it were no longer his. And then suddenly—he lost his bearings and sense of who he was entirely, feeling that he was falling into a dense cloud full of thunder and lightning.

When for whatever reason he somehow managed to ask about the backpack—he was answered by a woman's receding voice saying it served to carry bones and souls.

In the morning he woke up so exhausted that Anne could not get him up and out of bed until almost noon.

In the second dream, an Indian shaman-priest, shaking a gourd rattle, and his feet stomping the ground, and with copper jewelry clinking, sang to him of the spiritual Power, an energy that still circulated there, in what for hundreds of years was Cahokia—an energy that its ancient inhabitants had drawn down to the earth from the stars and the Gods and from the farthest reaches of the universe.

In another dream, the same shaman-priest passed to him his sacred, ceremonial pipe. And as the two of them took turns smoking it together, told him exactly where to excavate.

And in still another dream, he finding himself excavating by night with pick and shovel into the Holy Mound, broke through into a tunnel dimly-lit by a greenish glow that seemed to emanate from an unseen energy and that made his skin tingle.

He followed the tunnel. And soon came to a chamber lit up by the same greenish glow, only more intense, and where noiseless, wispy, bat-like beings hovered above a throne-like structure in which sat a robed man with Indian features who he could not be sure was alive or dead. Or neither. Two feather-like strips of copper were stuck into a bob of hair behind his head. Around his neck hung a pearl necklace, from which dangled, carved in precious stone, a human head. On his lap, two brown hands held a copper battle axe.

As if compelled, he went over, and his skin tingling like crazy, ever so lightly touched one of the hands. And in that very instant—was swallowed up by an explosion of blinding green light.

That woke him up.

He got out of bed and walked around the room squeezing his fists and doing deep knee bends, and at an open window stopped and looked out, and then up at the stars. After a while, he went back over to the bed, and nudging the sleeping Anne, told her he now had a Power that made him feel invincible.

She murmured, "Good—now maybe it will easier for you to move yourself out of bed in the morning."

And in three seconds she was again asleep.

The next night he dreamed that a fox jumped through an open window of the bedroom, and licked his feet.

The tickling woke him up.

Except that the fox, more exquisitely beautiful than he could ever have imagined a fox to be, was still there, just as before, but now looking straight at him with bright, steady eyes that seemed to penetrate to the core of his being. Raising her tail high, she said,

"To farm their corn—and sunflowers and amaranth and squash—they cleared the land—cutting down all the trees—even the ones bearing tasty persimmons—for firewood and buildings."

"They overpopulated everywhere with just themselves—making the Mississippi bottom lands unlivable for us foxes and for our deer friends and for all the other wild creatures as well."

"I'm very sorry to hear that."

"With no more deer—the elite—the high priests and their cohorts—had to have their cuts of deer meat brought to them from a hundred miles away."

"Tell me—what kind of life was that for the others?—not only digging from morning to night in the dirt to grow food to maintain and fatten the elite—but then also digging even more dirt—and more dirt and more dirt—and hauling it off on their backs—to erect the largest pile of dirt in the known world."

"I'm sorry for them too."

"The elite manipulated the ancient sacred ordering of the cosmos—wrote their own story—that legitimized their social distance from the people—that legitimized their right to exploit and control—"

"You don't have to say more—what you speak of is still happening—and as much as ever—everywhere."

With a hind paw, she scratched an ear. Then went on.

"The elite began to choke on so much deer meat and jewelry— and on their oversized monuments—and on their illusions of self-importance and power and superiority."

The fox raised her tail higher.

"Eventually—raiding the storehouses became the order of the day for outsiders—for those beyond Cahokia—and eventually became the order of the day for those within—for the disgruntled Cahokians—the hungry slaves—too."

"Stop—I know what you are going to say next—that anything like that deserves to crumble and topple—become rubble—except that piles of dirt that big can't—can only slowly wash away with the rains to muddy some more the waters of the Mississippi."

"That is exactly what I was going to say," she said—just before she leaped out the window and into the dark currents of the damp, East St. Louis night.

In the morning Paul told Anne,

"You know what?—I don't really have the Power I thought I did—because what I thought was Power wasn't Power after all—but only a perverse aberration of the human mind—meant for feeling superior and walking over others."

"I now see that when people who for more than a million years have lived as hunters and gatherers—settled down and stopped moving from place to place on two legs—there was a very big trade off—which was that genuine Power—their innate personal Power—rooted in caring for and not exploiting others—and in bringing joy—went asleep—went underground."

"And do you know what else?—I also see that it takes more than just a shaman-priest shaking a rattle to get it back again."

From the freeway, the screaming siren of an ambulance pierces Paul's brain and body—which attempting to defend themselves, stiffen, congeal.

Anne opens up a newspaper. After reading a while, she says,

"It says here they want to use the Cahokia mounds for sanitary landfills."

"You know what Anne?—nothing surprises me anymore—nothing."

A moment later he says, "I guess I was wrong about the nothing—because look—over there—the green buds on that tree—nature is still alive—and it looks like it's even going to be spring—would you believe it?—even here in East St. Louis—right in the middle of all this concrete and traffic."

"It's all in your head that you sometimes think you and everything around you is on the verge of extinction—why don't you read your new book?"

"If Cahokia disappeared in the blink of an eye—why not here?"

Paul sits there quietly for a while. Finally, opens his book—titled *River of No Return Wilderness*— and begins reading the introduction:

In central Idaho, three rivers—Big Creek, the Middle Fork of the Salmon, and the Salmon—twist and slide green and in places turbulent white though canyons which are among the deepest in North America.

This land of rattlesnakes, wild roses, and near desert down in the canyon bottoms and of alpine meadows and deep winter snows up high was once Indian—Sheepeater—which people lived mainly on the plentiful mountain sheep, elk, and deer, and on the salmon which came all the way from the Pacific and up those rivers to spawn.

Sitting under stars around their campfires—listening to the legends that bound them as a people, and to past hunts retold, and to the chirps of crickets and to the howling of wolves and coyotes, and to the rushing of the creeks and rivers—they thought life mostly good, and for that were grateful.

Above them the moon waned and grew round again for more than a thousand years.

And then, as if out of nowhere, like locusts, the White People came, homesteading and looking for gold, appropriating by the might of their guns the land, taking the fragrant forest, the sparkling water, the soft air, and even the sky from them, and from their children and their children's children.

Until only a handful of Sheepeaters remained.

Renegades they were called, whose last days were spent in minor and futile retaliations against the invaders.

In early summer of 1879, sixty mounted men of the Second Infantry with a long pack train, following moccasin tracks down Big Creek, were attacked at a narrows by rifle fire and forced to retreat up a hill. Pinned without water, they drank a keg of vinegar—before making a fifty-mile, forced march out of there, losing in their haste twenty-six loaded mules, some straying away and others rolling head over tail down the steep mountainsides.

In September of that same year, twenty three soldiers under Lieutenant Farrow pursued the renegades into the remote, rugged, mountains above the Middle Fork, destroying as they went the Indians' winter food caches.

Capturing two squaws, a boy, and a papoose, the soldiers sent one of the squaws back to her band, keeping her papoose, who cried all night. And when the next morning—fresh snow on the ground and bending the pines—Tamamo walked into the soldiers' camp, his white flag dangling on a stick, it was all over for fifty-one ragged, starving, destitute Sheepeaters, tired of fighting, tired of fleeing.

Paul looks up from his book and then down at the freeway, at the six, white, shining white lanes, and the sweeping, graceful curves of a cloverleaf.

And suddenly he feels sorry for them too—the ones passing by inside their wheeled, metal and glass containers.

He skips ahead in his book, and reads some more.

In 1907, as part of a national effort to exterminate the grey wolf from the West, a manual was issued to the Forest Rangers whose job it was to administer the Salmon River country on behalf of the American people. It instructed the Rangers how to poison, trap, and hunt the wolves, explaining such things as how to conceal the toothed, steel traps underground, and how to locate the spring wolf dens for the purpose of strangling all the pups except one, which then chained whimpering to a nearby tree, would lure in the other members of the pack.

The Rangers—aided by bounty and pelt trappers, and spurred on by livestock organizations, as well as by hunting and conservation groups that favored elk, deer, and mountain sheep—did their job. So that by 1930 only a few outlaw wolves remained, these for some reason often white in color, some with a mangled paw or missing toes—whose intelligence and indomitable spirit many of the old-time trappers came to admire more than the stuffy, constricting society that ordered their destruction.

He flips some pages.

Today that country is still relatively wild, in 1980 having been federally designated for preservation as the River of No Return Wilderness. A few salmon still make it past the downriver dams to spawn, and each spring the wild roses bloom. A few wolves have been reintroduced from Canada.

But of the Sheepeaters, only their pictographs and a few stone and bone artifacts remain. And a few place names—such as Farrow Mountain, Papoose Creek, and Vinegar Hill.

"Anne—I think I figured it out—the way I feel so much of the time—it must have something to do with feeling I'm a bit like the last Sheepeater—the last Indian."

He stares across the river, and beyond what was once Cahokia, far beyond, and with a strange look in his eyes.

"Or better yet—I think I feel like the last wolf—so maybe you should just call me Wolf—yeah that's it—Wolf."

Anne smiles.

"OK Wolf—if that helps any."

That evening, Wolf having curled himself wolf-like on the couch, says to Anne, who is kneading bread dough,

"The theme of the last chapter is that modern human beings—so totally surrounded by their gadgets and things—and trapped in their behemoth institutions—and caught up in the illusions and befuddlings of media-computer-consumer land—have lost touch with—have lost almost all recollection of who they really are."

11

He pauses, and then says, "They now accept boredom—and alienation and loneliness—as their natural condition."

Anne stops her kneading, and turning and smiling, says,

"You could have written the chapter yourself."

Wolf goes on.

"It says that people do not even suspect they are living lives that are inside out—they think their prison is freedom—their madness sanity—their immorality astuteness—their technology and knowledge and money personal Power."

"Possibly."

"What I think—is that a few of us need to return to the harmony and rhythms of nature—to the original Eden before the Fall—and there—from nothing begin again—and try to bring back for the others a vision of something better."

"You know—sort of like—do our part in putting America right."

He pauses, thinking hard—before saying,

"Maybe—return to someplace like the River of No Return country."

Anne again working her dough, says,

"Possibly—except that it might be easier—instead of going backwards—back up some River of No Return—to do that here in East St. Louis—in the world we know—and as it now is."

Wolf suddenly springs onto his feet and points.

"Damn it Anne—with your back turned you missed her—but a fox just ran by—and from the corner of her mouth spit out that society won't let you—will only laugh at you—"

"Or try to destroy you—even kill you."

Anne swings around with the ball of bread dough still in her hands.

"Anne—believe me—this fox is real—as real as it gets—and she knows."

"Knows what?"

"That life is not a casual game or pastime—and that sometimes it requires—just like in the old stories—that the Hero go off to a very far place—and by a long and difficult route—if he or she hopes to grab the New Fire from the Sun—that will save his people."

3.Why Not?

Living on the Navajo Reservation with his mother in a ramshackle trailer on the outskirts of Gallup, New Mexico, what Curly liked best was going with her to visit his grandparents whose home was a six-sided, mud-chinked, log hogan nestled among junipers and piñon pines and up against some smooth, red-rock cliffs at the foot of the Chuska Mountains.

There, always before the sun came up, his grandmother would call to him, "Wake up—arise—tidy and clean up around this hogan—so that the Gods of Dawn will know they are welcome here."

He could feel and did not have to be told that the hogan and the life that emanated from it was the center of an ordered Creation, where each thing, whether a stirring spoon or a piece of firewood, was sacred, had its special place and was to be respected and properly attended to. And where each thing was alive with Spirit—and was an indispensable part of the Whole.

He could feel and did not have to be told that from this very hogan emanated an intricate harmony of design that shone outward like a magic light in all directions across a beautiful and almost other-worldly landscape of colors and shapes and boundless sky—to as far away as the Four Sacred Mountains, and beyond. All of this making it possible for the Navaho—the People—to walk in Harmony and in Beauty.

He liked to scramble with his grandfather up the canyon behind the hogan to one of the old growth groves of towering ponderosa pines, many of them with trunks three and more feet thick and which his grandfather talked to, explaining to him that for the Navaho these trees too were grandfathers.

In one of those groves, he regularly participated in ceremonies which lasted for several days and in which Gods who could travel on rainbows and sunbeams were called down to bless, and to heal, and to assist the Navajo to walk in Harmony and Beauty and to journey long through life.

One time, the two of them gathering herbs, his grandfather pointed out to him, high up in the trunk of a pine, the nesting cavity of a Mexican spotted owl, explaining that the owls often steal their nesting places from ravens.

And also in these Chuska Mountains, his grandfather taught him to hunt deer the old Navajo way—explaining to him that before the

Navajo settled down to become farmers and sheep herders, they were hunters, and that it was the Gods who sent them game and guided their arrows—provided the hunter was worthy.

The hunt began with prayers in a sweat lodge, where he, his grandfather, and the other men, leaving behind the other, ordinary world, became transformed into alert, light-footed predators that saw and moved in ways that men without divine power could not. Afterwards, they rubbed their bodies with fragrant sage. And said more prayers:

> From home and with arrows I will travel.
> All around me the deer are gathering,
> And around me stand Holy People
> To guide my never missing arrow.
> The big buck is calling
> For the black bow—
> At the Holy Place.

After killing his first deer, and after carefully arranging its bones beneath a juniper tree, and again offering prayers, he said to his grandfather, "Our people should have remained wanderers and hunters— because that is who it seems we really are."

His grandfather said, "That is who the White People really are too—before they went astray—and lost all touch with what is most sacred and real."

Once he asked his mother, "Why do our old people have a seeingness and a sparkle in their eyes that White People do not?"

"Possibly—because they are not preoccupied with useless things—and because—they know."

"Know what?"

"Many things—but possibly mostly having something to do with being able to see past the wrapping of a thing to the thing itself."

"Whatever you say—and however much you may try to hide behind a false image—a mask—they always see you exactly as you are."

When his grandmother died, and soon afterwards his grandfather, Curly's world shrank back down to Gallup—with its silver and turquoise jewelry and Indian doll tourist stores, its pawn shops, and its too many addicts, whores, and drunks. Where his mother tried to hold life together with welfare checks and by cutting hair. But with a straightness to her back and with a spirit that could still be called a certain bearing, or dignity.

14

About a year later, visiting the abandoned hogan, he followed a freshly bull-dozed road—a bleeding, screaming gash of raw earth and uprooted trees and boulders. After a while, on the site of one of the sacred groves, he came upon a desolation of giant stumps and piles of tangled, green tree tops and branches.

That night, over a supper of mutton stew and canned peaches, his mother explained to him,

"What we see before us constantly twists and disappears in mysterious ways—to make room for the unraveling of something new— except that what is not there anymore is not really gone—it just seems that way."

One day, as he and the rest of his high school class, garbage sacks in hand, were being herded by their do-good White teacher—a *belagonna*—down a trash-strewn, rutted dirt road, all of them mechanically picked away at the beer cans, whiskey bottles, and plastic that the *belagonna* had told them now junked the grass and sagebrush landscape all the way to the Four Sacred Mountains.

However, it was not long before he and a few others were ranging far ahead and diligently hunting every bottle they could find, each discovered bottle making them frantic, scream and swear, as it was hurled and smashed on the nearest rock in the middle of the road.

Leaving a trail of sharp, broken glass—and them elated that they now had something to show for what they had thought would be just another stupid, wasted day.

In answer to the White teacher, he calmly said, "I was trying to destroy the Monsters."

"What monsters?"

"You know the ones you told us about?—the Giants who ravaged among us when the world began?—well, these are the ones you didn't tell us about—the ones the Hero Twins forgot to kill—or maybe it was because they being so misshapen—or not having any shape at all—the Hero Twins couldn't recognize or see them."

"Don't be a smart ass Curly—go pick up that glass."

A month later, at a squaw dance, and still no more than a little drunk, he picked a fight with another Navajo who was very drunk. With flailing fists, and cheered on by a small crowd, he beat the fellow bloody and senseless. He kicked once hard at the body lying motionless in the dirt. It not moving made him swear and kick some more—as others joined in, swearing and yelling and kicking at the heap.

He heard someone scream, "The son of a bitch is dead."

15

He grabbed a rock, and in one final effort—this time not trying to destroy indestructible Monsters anymore so much as to smash his way through to another reality—brought it down with both hands on the Navajo's chest.

In the Gallup jail, Curly's mother, as she turned to go, said, "When what was once the world is gone—where there now seems to be nothing—does not mean you are nothing—just that it becomes very difficult to tell where and how to begin again—where to place the first solid step."

She paused, then said, "It requires the seeing and courage of a warrior."

He studied for the GED. And ran in place for an hour each day—inspired by another story the White teacher had told the class, about how the young Hero Twins, switched with sticks by the Gods, were made to run around a mountain, and how eventually they beat those Gods in a race around the same mountain, pleasing them.

And he tried to make sense of his life.

Soon lost track of the days.

And then, by agreeing to attend the Navajo-run community college, and because the Navajo fully recovered, he was scheduled for early probation.

His mother told him, "I forgot to mention the most important part—about beginning again—and that is that the world is also full of allies who want to help you—and who will come to do for you what is most necessary—provided you learn to recognize them and treat them well—and let them."

At the college, he took some courses in Navajo history and religion. What particularly interested him were the healing ceremonies—Beauty Way, Mountain Way, and others—that cured by restoring in those who were sick a sense of being enveloped in the perfect Harmony and glittering Beauty in which the world began.

For a while he considered becoming a medicine man.

But he soon saw that with the free and independent life style of the hogan and its connection to the natural world almost gone, the old medicine would not work that well anymore—saw that the disarray, the alienation, and the sickness was simply too great.

He told his Navajo teachers,

"Just as the spotted owl takes its nesting place from the raven so have the Navajo always taken from neighboring people what was most useful—so it was with our horses and sheep—and rugs—and silver smithing—and so it is that I too want to listen closely to everything the world has to tell and show me—and to choose carefully—because why not?—why not from all that surrounds me create something that is new?—and harmonious and good?—even though it may not be quite Navajo."

One of the teachers said, "Without roots in a tradition or place—you may find yourself a very confused Navajo—a spirit floating alone in another universe."

Out of curiosity, he attended a Peyote meeting.

It took place in a hogan, where he and some other men, most of them dressed in Levis and cowboy shirts, and along with a few women, sat on mattresses spread in a circle around a low earth altar, in the center of which, on a bed of sage, was a fresh peyote top—Father Peyote. Alongside the God, a small pile of red, shimmering coals dispersed a sweet fragrance of cedar.

The peyote tea and the sliced peyote tops, passed around in enamelware pots, and the staff, eagle feathers, and sprigs of sage, the songs accompanied by the beating drum and rattling gourd, the quiet prayers and honest serious talk, the deep contemplation, the shrill eagle wing bone whistle blown four times, and finally, it getting light, the ritual breakfast of corn, meat, fruit, and water—

Made him feel whole.

And simultaneously part of a much greater Whole—that extended back to before time began.

The ceremony over, they all heaped paper plates with mutton ribs, fry bread, potato salad, canned peaches, and cookies, filled their cups with coffee, and ate and visited.

At one of those meetings he met Toma, a visiting Shoshone woman down from the Fort Hall Reservation in southern Idaho, who claimed to be a direct descendent of some Sheepeater Indians who had continued to live in the remote canyons of the River of No Return country for a number of years after the US government had announced it had rounded up the last of that renegade band.

She told him she was presently doing organizing work with a New Mexico environmental coalition trying to save the Chusca's old growth, ponderosa pine forests.

"I can't really explain it —my dedication to—my love for those trees—except that I know that they—those trees—and all the other plants too—and the animals that live with them—are somehow me."

17

"And that when you connect that closely to anything—it is almost a little like—well sex happening."

He went to more meetings.

Now and then, a switch began to click on somewhere inside him—that instantly brought him into a place luminescent with possibility and meaning.

A place beyond the reach of the White People or of anything else possibly wanting to destroy him.

And so—he began to travel the hard, Peyote Road. Whose obstacles, he saw, could be overcome by being a warrior, by walking with a straight back, and by right ethical living.

Nevertheless—he still sometimes got off onto the wrong fork. Or else just couldn't seem to get the switch to click on.

He told Toma that he now experienced in his heart what both his grandmother and grandfather had told him many times, but what had always been just words—that without the help of spiritual power, people are lost creatures.

When Toma suggested to him that his new spiritual power might also have something to do with their two bodies meshing so well together, and then went on to say that she wanted to take him back with her to the Fort Hall Reservation, and get married and raise some kids, he said,

"Huh—are you serious? —way up there?

"It's only a day's drive."

"Huh—but hey—the ancestors of us Navajo lived up in Alberta— and walked around on snowshoes— and then walked down into the Southwest—so sure—why not the Idaho Road?"

When his mother pointed out that the woman was not a Navajo, he said,

"We Navajo are already part Pueblo and Mexican—along with some White, Ute, and who knows what else—so why not a touch of Shoshone?—and anyway—I think I love her."

"You read too many books and see too many White People movies—to know anymore what is real—or good for you."

"We will help each other through life—through a very difficult dangerous world—be allies."

"That is very good—it may work then."

Waking up one morning, twenty years later, up on the Fort Hall Reservation, Toma rolls over on top of Curly and whispers into his ear that a raven had flapped into one of her dreams and told her that for her

18

to die with a light behind her eyes she needs to spend some time among the bones and spirits of her Sheepeater ancestors in the River of No Return country to the north of them.

"When I was a girl—my grandmother told me where the last few of them hid out—deep in a remote canyon not far from the Salmon River—I will take us to their cave."

"So—your raven friend thinks you need more than just me— huh—well I don't know about hobnobbing with bones—and having the spirits of the departed flitting around my head besides—but hey—the girls are in college—so why not the Salmon River?—why not the River of No Return Road?"

Curly beginning to pack, says, "How long do we go for?"

"The raven didn't say."

4. Government Mule

When Larry, on horseback and leading two heavy-packed mules, arrived for another season at his log cabin at Wapiti Meadow, deep in the River of No Return Wilderness, snow still lay scattered in heaps under the lodgepole pines and glacier lilies were poking up yellow.

At the far end of the June-green meadow, a herd of at least a hundred elk were quietly grazing, their new-born calves darting hither and thither.

A few days later, one of the mules took sick. Sitting by herself inside the pole corral, she looked as if she wanted to say something. So Larry spent time talking to her, at the same time scratching the insides of her long mule ears, which she loved, twisting her head for more.

Then suddenly one morning she was free of all struggle, of all movement and life—Sarah, the one who had always, with head down, kicked up her back heels at the stinging hail.

Shortly after first light, Eliot the District Ranger, dressed in crisp, Forest Service tan, and wearing a beige, straw cowboy hat, leads a tall sorrel mule over to his saddle horse Moon. Mounts, and with a tug on the mule's halter rope is off, smelling the early morning freshness and freedom of the forest.

Soon rides past a rustic, wooden sign:

**Entering
The River of No Return Wilderness
No Motorized Vehicles Permitted**

Swaying in the saddle to the clip clop of the stock on rock, he leaves the Ranger Station and road's end behind.

He excited— to finally be far away from it all.

Away from the eternal, deafening waterfall of policy and mandates cascading down from Washington and crashing and splashing down on his head— prescribing his every breath and move. Away from his every breath and move being watched and evaluated by those above him, who in turn are themselves being watched and evaluated. And so on up to the very top.

Soon is trailing down alongside Big Creek which rushes white, fast, loud, and brimming with the high country's snow melt. All around him, fat, yellowish, ponderosa pines thrust upwards and out of sight.

He not only excited, but happy as a bluebird.

A rounded yellow edge of sun appears behind a hill, its slant light filtering through the green needles of the ponderosa, and for just a brief moment the glint off his polished badge blinds him in one eye.

Straight ahead of him now is Vinegar Hill, blocking some of the cobalt blue of the sky.

At about five miles, at a brown, bear-mangled wood sign nailed to a tree, he turns onto the trail to Wapiti Meadow. And begins winding on tight switch backs steadily uphill.

The river now far below, he enters a forest of Doug fir— still climbing, clip clop, clip clop.

Climbs up still more.

Finally tops out. And winds down and up and around through tall, thin, lodgepole pines and across six small creeks.

The sun already high.

Larry is behind his log cabin, kneeling by the open door of a shed, also constructed of logs, and which is crammed full of tools and saddles and all the other paraphernalia having to do with horses and mules, repairing trails, and fighting forest fires. Piled beside him lie the tin cans he found several days ago hidden in the bushes behind one of last fall's hunter camps.

Swinging a short-handled sledge he smashes each one flat and sticks it into a burlap sack.

What earlier in the day had been mere puffs of cloud have mushroomed tall and billowy and dark-bottomed—splotching with dark shadow the green, lodgepole-thick hills.

He ties the sack shut, drags it inside the shed. Then returns and sits down against the trunk of a lodgepole pine, to relax as best he can with a few biting horseflies already in the air and the day promising lightning and possibly fires.

And also Eliot the Ranger—his boss—with a new mule.

Eliot, his feet dangling out of the stirrups to ease his sore knees, emerges out of the lodgepole pines and onto a green sprawl of meadow streaked blue with penstemons. Approaching the two log buildings and pole corral, he sticks his feet back into the stirrups and urges Moon on— the mule behind him arching his neck downward and tearing off big bunches of the meadow's new lush grass.

Trout in Wapiti Creek dart for cover as they approach, splash across.

He rides into the corral, and dismounting, hands Larry the mule's halter rope.

"His name's Sergeant."

Larry pats Sergeant's neck, and unhalters him—the mule turning and walking away and with head down sniffing the dirt of the corral.

"Thanks for bringing him—he looks like a real fine animal."

Eliot comments on the unusually fierce past winter, and the heavy spring runoff, and then as they head toward the cabin, describes in vivid detail the wiped-out sections of trail—the tangles of down trees, the washouts, the rock and mud slides.

"At times I wondered whether I'd even make it past some of those messes."

"Me too—coming into here even sure-footed Sarah stepped off into thin air and rolled somersaulting several times with her pack boxes clunking and clattering down into a rocky gully—it could have been that something got banged up inside her."

"Too bad—she was our best mule."

"Give me a week or so—and I'll have that trail all prettied up again—take all the high adventure right back out of it."

They enter the one room of the cabin.

Where Larry starts a fire in the stove, blows on it, sticks in more pieces of wood.

While he puts together and sets out a lunch of pan-fried trout, biscuits, coffee, and canned peaches—Eliot rambles on about the smoke the new man on Elkhorn Peak Lookout called into the Ranger Station several days ago. And which then Larry leading a packed mule rode off to.

But which neither he nor the spotter plane ever found.

Eliot rubbing both of his knees, says, "The fellow we got up there is a queer duck from back East—it always takes the new ones a while to tell smoke from ground fog."

Eliot as he returns from the outhouse pauses to admire the profusion of bear grass blooming like magical, surreal islets all around him: tussocks of longish, tough, grass-like leaves from whose centers slender green stalks rise up waist-high and terminate in huge, white, bell-shaped blooms—some of them having already been torn off and eaten by elk.

A brown, furry ground squirrel poised on its hind legs alongside one of the tussocks—scurries to its hole and disappears down into it.

Eliot remembers the squirrels, the tree squirrels he once hunted back in Arkansas—and the tasty stew his mother made with the ones he brought home and skinned.

And he remembers fishing for bass with his father from their leaky rowboat on a nearby lake—and them always catching enough to share with all the neighbors.

Remembers both of them talking about his dream of one day going out West and being a Forest Ranger.

But never did he dream that he, a Forest Ranger, would sit out most of his days dressed in spotless tan shirt and pants in a computerized office, neck-deep in meetings, phone calls, and studies and reports, and forever having to smilingly deal with tourists, miners, outfitters, environmentalists, higher-ups, and legislators—the resolution of one problem always seeming to create two new ones, such that there was no end to it and to the knot in the stomach it gave him.

Never did he dream that he would have to sneak away—as he is now doing—to smell his forest.

Thinking of Larry riding forest trails in whatever direction he chooses, the sun and wind on his face, and keeping fit and strong chopping out downfall and rolling out boulders, and with no one looking over his shoulder—he suddenly seethes with envy.

Larry—climbing out of the sack in the morning when he pleases.

That Larry, who never took a single forestry course, and not he Eliot, living the free and carefree life he once thought a Ranger's life would be.

What a Ranger's life used to be—years ago.

His sudden spontaneous swat squashes the horsefly on his wrist. With an index finger he flicks it away.

"Darn critters."

Eliot swings his sore bones back into the saddle.

"Probably won't get in here again for a while—I just don't seem to be able to get away anymore—like Sergeant there—penned in that corral."

"The trouble with you Larry—is that you have it too good back here—just you and the elk and the bear grass—and that you talk too much."

Larry shooing away a horsefly, says, "I may be showing up at the Ranger Station next week—I've already got a couple mule loads of trash that need to go out to the road—and on to town."

"I know—it's like it sometimes snows garbage back in these mountains."

Holding back the impatient Moon, Eliot continues.

"Even after twenty years it still amazes me some of the stuff that goes on back here—people doing what they well please—and to hell with anyone else and the environment."

He slaps at a horsefly on his neck and misses.

"And me— I'm handed this uniform and badge—and the job of keeping everything in order and everyone happy—and the elk and the bear grass too—why shoot."

Larry smiles, raises a hand in farewell.

And once again Eliot is joggling along. Clip clop, clip clop— across and then out of the meadow.

Then up and down and around through the lodgepole.

Clip clop, clip clop. Until before long, eventually overcome by the weariness of a long day of clip clopping and being joggled along—

Every tree, creek, and hill begins to look like every other.

Larry shoves more wood into the stove and fixes himself another cup of coffee.

He sits down with his coffee and to the reality of just himself back here. It strikes him that Eliot, having ridden off across the meadow and disappeared into the lodgepole, has ridden out of the world.

He muses over Eliot's comment about how some people are.

It crosses his mind that human existence, no matter how much it is bureaucratized and controlled, still remains, at bottom and for the most part, something random and unpredictable—and unknowable.

That human existence—is itself a kind of wilderness.

He hears a mule's long, loud, bellowing bray of anguish at being left behind.

Sergeant extending his neck, head and long mule ears over the corral gate, raises his head and brays again.

He wheels. And head still high, is now trotting circles. Halts abruptly before the gate, suddenly rears up, and balancing like some giant kangaroo—lunges smoothly over.

And never touched a pole.

A sharp crack of thunder startles Larry. He goes to stand by the window. To the east, a thunderhead, high-towering and dazzling white in the late afternoon sunlight is discharging lightning earthward—straight, hot yellow bolts, that stay blazing in the sky a while.

Seeing he may have to ride off to a real fire and not ground fog this time, he decides to feed his new mule some oats, check to see that the shoes are nailed on tight, scratch those long mule ears—then round up his horse and other mule.

Whistling, he steps into cool, moist air and walks toward the corral.

Which he sees is empty before he gets there.

Hard-hitting, freezing hail. Followed by a grey ocean of rain.

Eliot, hunched in the saddle, head down, body stiffened against the wet and the cold, huddles up to the glimmer of life still flickering inside him somewhere.

Huddles up to an image of himself already at the Ranger Station, beside a roaring, rumbling wood stove and in dry clothes—and forking into some hot peach pie.

The pain in his knees excruciating, he reins Moon to a stop and climbs off. Then leads him by the halter rope—the two of them splashing through the river of water gushing down what was once a trail.

Splash splash through the ocean of rain, he by now feeling himself utterly abandoned, helpless, powerless in the universe.

Nothing more than a servant, a cog, a tool—of who knows what.

The authority and power of the soggy man behind the brass badge a cruel joke.

When suddenly from behind—come thudding hooves and a mule's bellowing cry of greeting. And an instant later, Sergeant, hot-lathered with sweat and trotting with head high—abruptly slows to a walk at Moon's rump.

Moon whinnies.

As horse and mule clip clop and splash along together down the trail toward the Ranger Station and home.

5. Back to Eden

The Salmon River slides for the most part green, fast, and smooth. But here and there at rapids, such as at Growler, and at Devil's Teeth, it tumbles wild and white and frothy over gigantic boulders—these roaring turbulences of whirlpools and small waterfalls and powerful clashing cross currents having given rise to its other name, the River of No Return.

Along both shores, grass and brush-covered slopes dotted with a few scattered ponderosa pines rise abruptly a mile and more high—these the Salmon River Breaks, country so rugged it is seldom visited by anyone.

Wolf and Anne, as they climb a steep, rocky trail up through the Breaks, are studies in slow motion as they place one foot, then the other. Wolf is enjoying the hard exertion in the cool, sagebrush-scented morning. While Anne wonders whether she will ever make it out of this canyon—deeper than the Grand Canyon—much less though an entire summer.

Wolf stops to study his map, with a finger clears the sweat from an eye brow, and says,

"We should have crossed a creek by now."

They go on. And Wolf and Anne soon discover that no trail seems so impossibly long as when they should be there by now, but are not.

The hot sun pours down. Packs tug down on and cut shoulders, and legs hurt to lift. Ponderosa becoming more abundant, Wolf and Anne rest sprawled in their shade more than they walk.

Sitting against the thick, reddish trunk of a ponderosa that towers almost straight to sky before bursting into limb and needles, their heels dug into the dirt to keep from sliding, tumbling back down the mountain—Anne finishes the last of their three bottles of water.

She says, "What if the map is wrong?"

"We can always go back down to the river for the night—it's all downhill—and come back up in the morning—this time starting out earlier—and with more water."

She stares at him, unbelieving.

"An Indian—real life—doesn't rely on maps."

Wolf wiping the sweat from his forehead with a bandana, says, "For where the Hero has to go—there are no maps."

26

"Wolf—where the Hero has brought us—is pure hell—only hotter."

Higher and higher they climb, the last greenish arc of river below them gone—lost behind convoluted ridges.

And climb higher still—the heat now intense. Can barely push bodies and packs any more uphill.

When suddenly, the trail pitching abruptly downhill, knees begin braking, feet skidding, as they find themselves stumbling, delirious with expectation, into the bottom of a green, alder-choked ravine.

Whose creek, so thin they can easily step across, spills gurgling and clear across the trail and down the mountainside.

The Breaks, under the slant light of early evening, are tinged golden, the long shadows accentuating every rugged contour. And the air—the land fast losing its heat—is no longer hot, nor yet too cool. And extraordinarily still.

Wolf sitting somewhat apart from Anne, revives—begins to feel very good about their having made it up to this creek, this place. Overwhelmed by how perfect everything is.

"Anne—this could just be it."

"Could be what?"

"The right path—to the way everything used to be—to what the Golden Age of the old stories may have been pointing to—and the one about Eden too—before whatever it was disguised as a snake came down to Earth. "

Anne scrapes the last milk-soaked oat from her bowl. Takes some more dates.

"That food has to last a long time."

She puts the dates back. And says,

"If Adam and Eve—the children of God—could not do it—nor the Cahokians with their magic and ceremonies for renewing the worn-out world—why then us?

After a very long pause, Wolf says,

"Because—because we are not them."

Two days later, now out of the ponderosa pines and in the high country, Wolf wanders by himself through cool, green, lodgepole forest, navigating between tussocks of rain-wet bear grass and waist-deep in a sea of their large, white, bell-shaped blooms.

27

He catches sight of a black bear. Which more imposing and startling in its aliveness than anything he has ever before experienced, rears up tall on its hind legs, and for a brief instant, seems to be admonishing him, like a stern father or grandfather—before wheeling and galloping off through the pines.

A moment later, he spots an elk thistle, a spiny plant with coarse, pale purple flowers. Stooping, hunting knife in hand, he cuts the stalk. *Boiling will soften the spines*, the book had said, *making a very tasty green.*

He heads towards another thistle.

Anne hiking along far behind, ruminates about last evening.

When she had suggested they put up a solid shelter against what looked to her like imminent rain, Wolf answered that there were still stars out, and that he wanted nothing between himself and them blazing overhead.

The storm, which blew in about midnight, drove them under an overturned Doug fir, its three-foot-thick trunk high enough off the ground to give some protection to their heads and shoulders. And draping a nylon tarp over their sleeping bags, they waited out the rain like that—wet and shivering.

Anne stops for a while to watch a red-shafted flicker at its hole in a lodgepole pine, the bird dipping its long beak in and out of the chirping, gaping mouths of its young.

Sets off again.

What she wants from him—wanted—will never happen. How tired she is of him taking so little account of her, who could be almost anyone tagging along. Back in East St. Louis, she had assumed that their life went by too furiously and fast, that people bothered him too much, and that the distractions were too many, for him to ever really see her, to be fully present with her.

And how tired she is of his intensity, this new intensity that seemed to have grabbed hold of him right after his dream encounter with the Corn Maiden.

She realizes she had been a fool to agree to this fool's errand—to have thought that tromping through the wilderness for a summer would change him.

She mutters, "Paul—Wolf—Hero—I am tired—exhausted."

"And I am even more tired of you wanting to make me feel that everything you think is important matters so much—and is also important for me."

When she comes upon Wolf, he is kneeling in the trail and feeding sticks into a small fire he has built between two flat rocks which support a blackened, steaming pot.

"I've had it Wolf."

Wolf picks up a stick and stirs his thistles.

Still stirring, he says, "Life—its evolution—is what emerges out of struggle—and out of all the mistakes and setbacks and dead ends—there is always opposition—particularly whenever one reaches for anything really new—give this a chance."

"I'm sorry Wolf—but that's not the problem—I'd like enough of the food to last me back down to the river."

"At least first taste these greens—they're delicious—I'll make some tea too—then see what you think."

She watches the hand, now stirring more vigorously, almost frantically.

And it strikes her that a part of him is further away than ever—or perhaps even missing entirely—just like after his adventure with the Corn Maiden, when for at least a week he was either in a dead sleep or else stumbling around the house as if in a cloud.

He abruptly stops stirring his greens.

And looking up toward her, says, "Do you remember the Corn Maiden I told you about?"

Anne blinks several times.

"The woman with the backpack?—with the snake camped on her head?

"Her."

"I never told you this—but knowing her did something to me—for a while it was like the whole universe was exploding—and surging through me and lighting me up—and then—the very moment she disappeared—it was as if I was nothing—in a world of nothing."

"It just could have been—that she made off with my Soul."

She is acutely aware that whoever or whatever he is seeing, talking to, it is not her.

"And wandering by myself through this luscious blooming bear grass—gathering elk thistles—and seeing that bear—all that

29

excruciating aliveness—screaming at me—made me realize how much I wanted it back"

He pauses, before saying, "Not only every last bit of it—but much more too."

"Because I now see that before the Hero can do anything—anything at all—he or she needs to be sound and whole."

"And so—maybe I need to find her—the Corn Maiden."

6. Bushman of the Kalahari

When Stephanie had suggested what she referred to as open marriage, Peter did not object, that is not until she began to prefer someone else to him, wanted to leave him and her comfortable life for an unpublished poet. But by then nothing he said or did could hold her, which put his superbly ordered world into such shambles he could barely struggle to a restaurant twice a day to eat the meals to stay alive, much less design space probes for NASA. A friend, tired of hearing him wallow in self-pity, suggested he go up on a fire tower to rethink and rebuild his life.

A month later, taking three months leave without pay, and with a job on a fire tower that promised peace, time to think, and enough routine to keep from going mad, Peter drove west.

At the Ranger Station, he was put on a horse, and his trunk, crates of food, and box of books lashed on mules. Then he and the cowboy packer wound uphill and down, for what soon became for him a blur of endless, hard miles, the final switchbacks so steep that the stock—white-lathered, snorting, and breathing hard—stopped every fifty yards to rest.

The lookout at last—not sticking up high in the air on a tower as he had been expecting, but merely a wooden cube painted white and glassed on all four sides from waist level to the eaves and perched on a pile of rocks.

The packer, when he got back to the Ranger Station with the stock, told Eliot that it looked like they had a good man up there on Elkhorn Peak.

"Told me he got tired of shooting rockets off into space and needs a vacation to fallow his brain."

Peter marks off on the calendar the beginning of his 27th day on the mountain.

He sticks another piece of wood into the fire box of the crackling wood stove, and then carefully lays three pieces of French toast on the griddle upon which sizzling strips of bacon are beginning to curl. Slipping on his glasses, he steps outside, where he quickly scans the forest in all directions—near and far. But finds no wisp of smoke, no fire to report. Going back inside, he turns the bacon and French toast, clicks on the radio, and calls the Ranger Station.

31

When Eliot finally answers, Peter tells him he sees no fires this morning, and they sign off.

Peter arranges his golden French toast, perfectly crisp bacon, and some squares of margarine on a large white plate, and flooding everything with syrup, sits down to breakfast. Alternating bites of French toast with bites of bacon and sips of Oolong tea, and looking out his picture window, he is aware that this for him, even without real butter, is simply the best part of the day.

He listens as Jane—whose lookout glints on the skyline 10 miles away—calls Eliot to let him know she sees no fires this morning.

Peter lights up at the sound of Jane's voice, a voice throaty and moist and thicker with sexuality than any he has ever heard. And suddenly, a crazy idea of her mouth driving him half crazy, he wants to abandon his French toast and dash across the green, stick-backed sea of valleys and ridges to her.

Eliot, his voice brightening, asks her how it is going up there on Diablo Mountain, and whether she has heard any wolves howling. She says she loves lookout life, and yes, she heard some howling two nights ago—an eerie, beautiful music, which absolutely thrilled her—and then she and Eliot chat excitedly about the tragedy of the earth's vanishing species.

"Damn that ranger—he's doing it with her right over the radio."

Striding along in mountain boots and tan canvas shorts, a rucksack on his back, Wolf, sun-swart and with the beginnings of a beard, is roaming the wilderness, free as a bird.

Lingering where he pleases—a minute or a day.

Having left the rubble of America falling down—miles behind.

Peter thinks about Stephanie.

That it is his lucky star she is gone, she who had resisted with stubborn, woman's pride and with stupid, illogical defenses his every rational, sensible, and practical suggestion.

Poor, beautiful Stephanie, the hopelessly romantic, anthropology graduate student, against whom one could only rage.

For whom open marriage was but a ruse for sleeping with her word-slinging, poet friend, he as misinformed and deluded about life as her.

He sits down on his cot. Reaches for the book she gave him as a going away present—*Bushmen of the Kalahari*. And begins to read.

A willow pole across his shoulder, Wolf walks across a meadow in places matted down where elk have recently bedded down. Dropping to his knees, he sneaks up to a thin, deep-running brook. And bringing the pole back and forward, flips a horsefly onto the water—and immediately pulls out a flashing six-inch trout.

He crawls upstream to undisturbed water—and catches another.

Peter sits in the outhouse with the door wide open, looking out at the mountains—the highest one, on the horizon, Diablo.

His thoughts wander back over eons to the primordial soup—whose first viruses and bacteria gave rise over time and ever so gradually to increasingly complex creatures, and finally to him, Peter—and to this computer and space-age world.

It is clear to him that just as the earth seems to be getting along fine without wooly mammoths and dinosaurs, so would it probably also manage quite well without wolves—and without whatever other creatures that are unable to cope with the new environmental conditions in which they continually find themselves.

The trout, wrapped in mud and baked in coals, then eaten hot with the fingers, are delicious.

Still hungry, Wolf eats a few peanuts and dates—realizing that unless he sets a snare on some well-used game trail and strangles an elk or a deer, he will, by fall, be thinner than a lodgepole pine.

Peter sits at his table munching cheddar cheese and crackers and sipping apple juice—eating slowly. Because ten minutes later, lunch over, he does not know what to do next.

He wanders outside and climbs onto the roof of the lookout, where removing his shirt, he lies face down to sunbathe in the thin, cool air. But not even the pleasure of a warm sun beating on his back can lull away the dullness, the desperate eagerness for an event—a forest fire, a visitor, anything to overturn the day after day sameness of life on top of this mountain.

Sitting up to look for fires, he sees a lone cow elk walking up the trail that leads down to his spring. She sniffs the ground. Then drops stiffly onto her front knees, and her hind end collapsing, the head rocking back, sits there in the sun, totally at ease, her large ears high and spread wide.

"Why can't I do that?—just hang out up here—and find my bliss."

Peter lies back down—closes his eyes.

An image wells up in his mind of small, brown-skinned Bushmen running a wild antelope-like animal to exhaustion across the African desert, along with images of sand and rock, patches of tall grass and thorny bushes, an occasional muddy water hole, and a burning, endless sky.

For a brief moment he marvels at how early human beings, naked to heat, cold, biting insects, and ravenous, sharp-toothed beasts that prowled at night, managed by their wits and toil to fill their bellies and raise families and to survive for more than a million years.

Tries to imagine a life without science and books—or French toast.

Feeling thankful for the impetus toward something more, toward the civilization that has passed the harsh and pitiful life in nature by, feeling almost blessed, chosen, a proud member of the technological elite—Peter falls asleep.

Wolf picking up a dented, white enamel coffeepot dips it in the Elkhorn spring, and head back, gulps ice-cold water, some of which dribbles down his bare chest.

He continues uphill, and noticing fresh footprints, perks up at the prospect that whoever is manning the lookout just might, in good backwoods tradition, invite him to supper—and who knows, maybe to breakfast too.

A crashing in the timber wakes Peter—who sits up.

Seeing a back packer where the cow elk had been, coming up the trail—he quickly pulls on his shirt. Scrambles down off the roof.

Then stands there beside his woodpile, waiting—expectant.

Wolf looking fresh and rugged, as if he might eat mountains for breakfast, strides up to him, and not even removing his pack, says,

"I jumped an elk back there—man—talk about effortless grace—the way she bounded off and over high logs—seemed to make the whole forest itself leap up and come alive and dance with her."

Peter always amazed by how soon he can tell whether someone is or is not his type, it immediately strikes him that this bare-chested Viking—with his swagger, sunny good looks, and poetic sentimentalism—is definitely not.

34

Wolf looking off at the far peaks, fixes on Diablo on the horizon. And says,

"Some view you have up here."

Peter says, "Yeah— from high up a person can see a long way."

"People out there just don't realize how much they still need something like this—what you have all around you."

Wolf slides off his pack, it thudding onto the ground at his booted feet. Again looks off in the direction of Diablo, before turning back to look at Peter.

"Because what I'm learning every day back here—and in spades—is the extent to which civilization—in order to exist—has sabotaged—driven underground almost all of what was once most human—most innately us."

"Which could be why people nowadays seem so empty—filling up their lives doing and believing nutty stuff—and then seeing themselves as the epitome of sophistication besides."

Peter begins to feel very superior, and again, very chosen—as he recognizes in the whining of this Viking, this Neanderthal standing before him, something akin to the crazed despair and mad thrashing of the last dinosaurs, before they went extinct.

Wolf vaguely aware that something about Peter, his increasingly odd demeanor, seems to be spurring him on, continues.

"People are beginning to acknowledge their destruction of the earth—but so far are blind to their own and much greater psychic destruction."

Peter, smiling weirdly, says,

"It could all be as simple as that some people are unable to adapt to and deal with the new realities of modern existence—it having been their bad luck to have inherited too many genes that were maybe once useful— but that now only get in the way—which is why 98 % of all known species are extinct. "

Wolf spits out, "Or it could be that those very genes are the only ones still capable of restoring the human center to a world that has gone awry."

Wolf amazed at how quickly he fell into this conversation, nevertheless continues, his jaw tighter even than before.

"Or that failing—look at the ruins of the Byzantine and Roman Empires—and what was Imperial England—it could just be that those genes will nevertheless prevail in other ways—leaving nothing but twisted girders sticking up from the rubble."

Peter takes a step backwards, suddenly frightened by this madman. Hears himself swallow hard.

Hears the madman rail on.

"Civilization—modern society—in its mania to control—in stuffing everyone and everything—all neatly boxed and labeled and recorded—into one big squarish master box— "

Peter mumbles, "Every culture—even the Kalahari—is a box."

Barely makes out the words, as Wolf says,

"Except that in those older cultures—the so-called backward ones—what was always most important—sacred—was to regularly break out of the boxes—to transcend them and their flimsiness and the mental illusions that kept them pasted together."

Wolf wanting desperately to escape the stiff, ill wind he seems to have stirred up and which seems intent upon sweeping him right off this beautiful mountain top—bends over and begins to adjust a strap of his pack, as he says,

"By the way—what's the trail over to Diablo Lookout like?—anybody up there?"

Peter, his eyes glazing, hears himself again swallow hard.

And almost chokes on the image of this drunk-on-himself barbarian and Jane pressed naked together on her narrow government cot.

"Hey—I asked you a simple question."

But Peter now sees standing before him only an unpublished poet, who flitted with such passion and eloquence into the life of Stephanie that she deemed his clever string of words real and wonderful—abandoning herself to them and to him completely.

"Look at yourself—I could knock you over just blowing on you—is anybody up there?"

Peter by now too crushed to be scared, mutters, very faintly,

"Possibly."

Wolf jerks his pack back up onto his shoulders and strides off into the trees—toward Diablo Lookout, glinting like a beacon of salvation on the horizon.

Peter, his world in shambles, does not know what to do.

Wanders dazed, tripping once on a rock, back into his coop. Sinks down onto his cot.

Sits there.

Now staring down at the naked Bushman on the cover of the unfinished book alongside him.

Little by little, from out of the haze, at first very vaguely, and then with increasing clarity, it occurs to him to bushwhack down to Dismal Creek, far down below him, and far from a trail, and possibly unreached by any white man ever.

Taking with him—absolutely nothing. No pocket knife or food. Not even a match—or single candy bar.

Poised silent and motionless by a pool, arm cocked and holding a long, pronged wooden spear, he will ambush a trout. Twirling wood against wood he will generate heat for a glowing ember, which nursed onto finely-shredded bark, he will blow into flame. And roast his fish over hot, glowing coals.

And with the coming darkness, he will wrap himself to sleep in fir boughs.

He sees it is only half past two. He gets up and takes one last look for fires. Flicks off the radio. Again smiling weirdly, but this time even more weirdly, and now more weirdly still, he strips naked, except for his glasses.

Then steps, hesitantly, barefoot into the wilderness.

7. All of Creation

Peter as he worked his way upstream, speared not a single trout—only glimpsed them darting out of sight beneath the bank.

Instead, pushing through a patch of willows, he slipped in some mud and pitched into a moose bog. Where limbs flailing to keep the lank naked body from vanishing forever in the green and yellow slime—he lost his glasses, the world about him just like that shrinking to half of what it had been.

That night, tucked under heaped-up pine needles, he slept hardly at all, missing like never before the warm, live body of Stephanie—she once the light in the dark night of his soul.

When he woke up to a sleek fox stepping into a patch of moonlight, and who gazed at him for a long intense moment, and then disappeared—afterwards, he was not sure whether he had dreamed it.

The first hint of an unusually blurry dawn suggests to Peter that odd state without substance which quantum theory posits as a constantly fluctuating sea of the infinite ways in which it is possible for subatomic particles to actualize.

Each particle living out all of its possibilities—most of them contradictory—simultaneously.

Until a conscious observer, someone like him, Peter, equipped with the necessary intellectual and sensory apparatus, singles out a particle and also one of its infinite number of dynamic attributes for attention—and makes a measurement.

In which instant, out of what before seemed nothing, only a swirling hodgepodge of possibilities, one of those possibilities actualizes, leaps into what is called existence—taking on the structure, the illusion of unshakable bedrock reality.

He grudgingly acknowledges that the back packer was right. What people think of as real—is something very insubstantial and tentative.

He stands up, and brushing some clinging pine needles from his body, takes his first step uphill—already exhausted.

He takes another step, and another, and more steps, struggling as if against some torrential river of no return up the steep mountain—knowing that even in an indistinct world, uphill will lead him to the top, and that on top is his lookout.

After a while, he says aloud, "Except for the glasses—I sort of came out of this not half bad."

All around him rise ponderosa pines, their huge trunks in the slant light of early morning golden and towering upward, as if surging up out of another world.

They remind him of another people, perhaps from another universe, an alien race of strange giants greeting the new day in a language he does not understand.

It occurs to him that once two subatomic particles have interacted, whenever only one of them is then measured, it has an instantaneous effect on the other—no matter how far the two are apart.

Which could mean, he suddenly realizes, that a part of him is, at some cosmic level, inextricably connected to those ponderosas, does in some fashion understand their language after all.

Moving upward, and up some more—he ascends a mountain that seems steeper and higher than he remembers coming down.

He looks ahead of him for the first lodgepole pine that indicates he is getting close.

But only finds himself surrounded by more ponderosa, they ever more dense and surreal—their massive trunks now, in the brilliance of late morning, slowly dissolving into pure shimmering goldenness, into pure shimmering energy.

Up ahead, in the midst of where the goldenness is most dazzling, and out of that very goldenness, something very large begins to take on form, and reality—as it pushes upwards.

A flattish square-like something—and then on top of it another just like it, and another. Then another.

Just like—just like a stack of—perfectly golden French toast.

Down whose sides begin to cascade thick, silent, slow rivers of syrup and melted butter.

The stack soon towering higher than had any ponderosa.

Drawing Peter, his fatigue gone, upwards, and upwards, to what just might be—Heaven.

Who now sees that the huge stack of French toast is sitting right on the top of his mountain.

But which stack, as he tops out, takes his first joyful step into Heaven, vanishes—poof—back into the quantum nothingness.

Leaving where it had been nothing but a jumble of jagged, grey rock. And, a solitary, dark-skinned—Kalahari Bushman.

The aborigine, his coal-black hair hanging to just below his shoulders, is sitting motionless sideways to Peter in the shade of a boulder. He is wearing a tawny, leather breech cloth and moccasins of the same material—and has a short, sinew-backed bow and several arrows across his lap.

He, with the help of Talking God, has been hunting White Men—those the Lakota refer to as the Takers Of The Fat, and who have everywhere like the very devil's weed infected and fouled the Earth Mother Spirit.

Over this and that mountain have already flown more than a hundred sharp-pointed arrows—plock plock into the unfeeling hearts and confused out-of-whack brains of the mortal enemy.

Plock—plock—plock—plock.

The arrows never giving out—as they fulfill their heroic and Holy Mission.

The aborigine remaining motionless, Peter says, "You there—what happened to my French toast?—and how did I get to Africa?"

Head and the black mane of hair whirl toward the disturbance.

Eyes lock onto the naked, white body totally disconnected from That Which Blows Breath Into the Creation—pitiful in its absurdity and loneliness.

Its longish dong dangling between white, hairy legs.

The aborigine—crazy-eyed—readies his bow, to put the next arrow right there. Draws the arrow to his ear.

Peter yells, "And where is my lookout? —it was here yesterday?"

Which voice this time snaps the aborigine wide awake. Blinking several times, and very confused, he lays the bow and arrow down alongside him—then stands up, and unable to keep from laughing, says,

"This is truly incredible—and just who or what might you be anyway?"

"My lookout—and where did you learn English?"

The aborigine for a moment puzzled, finally says, pointing,

"The only lookout is that one across the valley from us—on what some call Elkhorn Peak."

Peter who cannot see that far, and by now not able to tell whether it is he that is spinning or the world that is spinning about him, says,

"Oh."

"Almost all of us Navajo speak English."

"What are you hunting?—it's not hunting season."

"A fat mountain sheep to eat—they hang out and lamb in these rocky cliffs—here on the land of my wife's people it is always hunting

40

season—it is said that very long ago some of their women went off to live with the animals and mated with them—and in doing so they established a special pact with those animals—that is forever."

"This is government land—Forest Service land."

"That may well be what some say—however, this land was taken from my wife's people with guns and trickery—more or less exterminating them."

"They were Sheepeaters—a mountain band of the Shoshone—a humble and gentle people who had been living here—hunting and gathering and fishing for salmon and having children—for thousands of years."

The aborigine pauses.

"And so it was for us Navajo too—and for the people of every other sovereign, indigenous nation—for every square inch of what came to called America—what came to be known as the land of the rights of the individual—and of equality—and of freedom and a better life for all."

The spinning stopping, Peter suddenly finds himself with his bare feet solidly planted on this rocky mountaintop. And as he begins to assimilate in its entirety and essence the blurred presence before him— he, Peter, senses that he may be beginning to see in a way he never quite has before.

Speaking with words and feeling that strike him as having their origin in some other very far-off place, he says,

"Yes—a continent strewn with tens and tens of thousands of slain and bleeding foxes—and the White invaders from Europe knee-deep in red rivers and pools of blood—and smiling and laughing—as they bestowed upon themselves a Venerable Constitution as well as the indisputable land titles that made it all legal and honorable."

"Just as abducting black people out of Africa was."

The brown man is stunned, does not know what to make of this crazy, gawky, naked White Man. Who seems to have acquired—and just like that—what seems like it just might be Sight. Power.

A strange, powerful Power—that seems to be engulfing him too.

Because off to one side of this naked White Man, up in the sky, he sees the ancestors of the Navaho, migrating in small bands from far in the snowy North down into the sun-drenched Southwest, and there, they too killing and taking lands by force. Hears the Hopi referring to his people as Head Pounders.

41

And then, off to the other side of the White Man, he sees in the sky the bands of mounted, young Navaho warriors, trained from birth to kill, descending upon, raiding the Pawnee—taking horses and women and slaves. And doing the same far down into Mexico.

The visions, in a blink of the eye, gone—he continues to stare at what is now blank blue sky.

Speaking very softly, he says, "I see that in this Creation which grants me my existence—everything plays its necessary part— even famines—epidemics—dishonor—brutality—and the White Man—who with his arrogance and conquering technology some of us Navaho see as strangling everything that for us is most noble and good."

He pauses.

"My grandfather would tell me—do not complain—do you want a forest without dead dry branches for firewood?—or without rotten stumps—with golden pitch at their centers for starting the fire?"

He stares more intently at the sky—and then, beyond it.

"I see that everything is very much a Mystery—and that it is to that impenetrable Mystery we must always speak and pray—but without words."

Peter finds himself thinking about how whenever one attribute of a sub atomic particle is perfectly known, its conjugate attribute becomes invisible—unknowable.

From which it must follow that even with the whole of science, one does not even begin to know the fullness, the essence of anything.

Hears a voice saying, "But tell me—why do you wander about away from your lookout?—and plucked-bird naked as you are."

Peter stands there a while, as if thinking.

Finally says, "My wife left me."

"Consider it your good fortune you no longer live with someone who does not want to live with you—there are many good women."

"My people lost everything—the grass and the animals and the wind—as well as the stories that held the world together."

"I could answer that for me she was my herds of buffalo—and the wind waving the sweet prairie grasses—but you are certainly right—the devastation for your people was much more total—I mean how and where for you and them to even begin?"

"Like—can one even still be an Indian?"

"My grandmother told me that everything that is most Indian came out of living outdoors in nature—and having almost nothing."

"And most Indian—is what?"

Some say it is correctly performing the obligatory rituals—some say it is knowing a freedom that no White Man can even begin to imagine—and having a close warm kinship with the animals and with those of one's clan—and walking strong and in Beauty through a landscape impregnated with our sacred stories and legends."

"And some might say that what is most important is journeying regularly to the Other World which lies behind the one we think we see—to remind one that one's Being—one's Soul—one's Power— who one really is—is rooted there."

"And for you?"

For me most Indian was eating fry bread made with the white flour and lard and the sugar we bought at the White Man's trading post—and growing up having some good times under a blanket with a cousin."

They both laugh, as the brown man says,

"Huh—I mean what is anything?"

Peter sensing himself being drawn by some invisible, cosmic force field and ascending, this time without effort, as if up some river of no return to its source, again hears himself speaking, again from that same far off place.

"Up until the dawn of agriculture on this Earth—my ancestors too roamed in nature with almost nothing—so I too—in spite of what I might appear to be—no matter how laughable—must still have flowing inside of me their blood and Spirit."

"Then you and I may be brothers—come Brother—I will take you to your lookout—there are sheep trails we can follow."

The words from Peter now an unstoppable torrent.

"And if one goes back far enough—my ancestors were the foxes—and all the other animals—and before that the trees and other plants—and before that the rocks—and the sun and the moon and the stars—so all of Creation must be my brother too."

"Come along now—so that night does not catch us."

And the brown man grabbing his bow and arrows, they set out, two aborigines, down a grey rocky ridge. The fast pace over rocks hurts Peter's bare feet, but he, feeling himself a warrior, enveloped in he knows not what, and invincible, does not complain.

He shouts, "Who needs it?"

The brown man stopping and turning, says,

"Huh?—who doesn't need what?"

43

"A beautiful woman with a prestigious graduate degree—a fancy town house—French toast—quantum theory—being chosen to lead the way to the stars—any of it."

"If you'd hush—we may surprise some sheep."

8. The King

Cowboy hat tilted slightly down for style, .357 magnum hanging at his hip and ready for bear or whatever, but mostly too for style, Al, big game outfitter and guide, in the cool, freshness of this morning, is riding his Appaloosa mare along the open, grass and sagebrush-covered crest of Cold Mountain Ridge—leading and sometimes yanking along a packed buckskin reluctant to walk so fast. Here at 7000 feet, the sky is such an intense blue that Al knows he could touch it. In front of him and to both sides, he can see for twenty miles.

Nothing but a green undulation of ridges, peaks, and valleys—with the loftiest portions still under snow and glistening white.

For Al the lover of freedom and Lebensraum it is nice country to be riding tall and high in the middle of, smelling the sage, left hand loosely holding the reins, the other the buckskin's lead rope, and being transported effortlessly and only now and then having to touch his spurs to the flanks of the Appaloosa laboring and occasionally snorting beneath him.

On such a fine morning, in such a place, a man feels very alive, just wants to ride, ride, ride—is King.

He drops down into a saddle. There, where a weathered wood sign nailed to a tree says Four Way Junction, he turns north and begins to descend, clattering down off the ridge. And soon is winding among tall, sky-piercing Doug fir, whose two and three-foot thick trunks rise up from an uncluttered ground cover of pine grass and fir needles.

Al does not know which he likes better, the intimacy of this open, sunlit, park-like forest or the horizon to horizon expansiveness of the high ridge he just came down from—only that upon riding out of either of those worlds it always thrills him to find himself so suddenly and as if by magic in the other.

Traversing down and around a steep sidehill, he comes upon three down Doug fir, overturned by the blasts of last winter's winds, and now lying in a tangle of trunks, roots, and branches across the trail. To go around, he spurs the Appaloosa sharp right up the steep slope, the two animals snorting as their haunches drive frantic hooves into the loose rock avalanching downward under them. Passing above some roots thrusting skeleton-like out from the base of one of the trunks, the buckskin breaks away, and Al curses when the animal stays put.

But which then whinnying, lurches ahead, following along behind—buckskin and Appaloosa skidding back down onto the trail in another avalanche of loose rocks.

The miles go by. And as the day warms up, and begins ever so slightly to drag, Al's mind wanders back to last fall:

Snowing a blizzard and with frozen hands having to redo a string of six pack horses which panicking, each one pulling on the others, had tumbled rolling together down the mountainside—pack saddles and packs all over the place and one packhorse wedged with its legs in the air against a tree.

Following the blood trail of a dude's gut shot elk into downfall so thick it took him and the wrangler all day to wrestle the quarters over logs crisscrossed five feet high and out to where they could be packed onto the stock.

The doctor who rode Joker—the outfit's best horse—out to Black Butte, where he tied him to a tree and then took to the timber gun in hand, getting his elk all right, except that when he ran whooping to the downed animal it turned out to be Joker lying there stone-dead and still tied to his tree.

Al laughing, says aloud, "Why shi-it—who says all the adventure has gone out of life."

Larry bent forward in the saddle, and leading a packed mule, winds his way up the switchbacks to Four Way Junction. Stuck under the cargo ropes that hold together the mule's two mantied packs and easy to get at are a long crosscut saw, an ax, a pick-mattock, and a shovel.

Coming upon a boulder that has rolled down from above and onto the trail and that reaches to his horse's chest, he dismounts and ties up to a tree. Finds a long pole—and then using a rock for a fulcrum, levers an edge of the boulder upward, it rolling bounding and crashing down the mountainside.

Back in the saddle, and giving a tug on the mule's lead rope, he continues toward Four Way Junction.

Al relives in his mind some of what he has countless times told his dudes when in the evenings all of them would sit around the table in the cook tent sipping beers and whisky and swapping stories:

"You guys have come out here to do what every free man worth his salt used to always do—which is hunt—hunt hard and smart—go out after the critters in any weather until he got one—and then bring home the meat to the lady and the kids—and she real appreciative at night under the covers."

"That's what life was all about—you better believe it."

"Now—with the Forest Service—the government—Big Daddy—chipping and chipping away at a man's independence—his freedom and dignity—his very identity—all of that is almost gone— and it's another kind of bird entirely—making any outfitter sick enough to want to saddle up—pack the ol' mule—and head off into the setting sun."

"Why nowadays—with chainsaws banned—they tell me I have to saw firewood—and I mean cords of it—by hand with a whip saw— and then afterwards saw off the stumps at ground level—nose to and knuckles scraping the dirt—to make them invisible—to preserve wilderness aesthetics."

"Horseshit—when what really matters is being a man—a human being—you guys understand that?—being able to go out in any direction whenever you want—being allowed to piss wherever you find yourself."

"That government bureaucrat Eliot strutting around like a big-shot peacock Ranger—why there's no man left in him—he's nothing but a god damn walking badge and rule book."

"When the sonofabitch rode into camp waving a sandwich wrapper and preaching to me about litter—I said to him—listen here Eliot—it wasn't us—because I tell my fellows to turn in every single wrapper or else they don't get a lunch sack tomorrow—which shut him with his rules and regulations up good."

"But the saddest part is that these days it's the same or worse everywhere—the pressures to shape up—do this do that—the nosey surveillance—and the humiliations at every turn—and to top it off—people don't even know anymore what has happened to them."

"I tell myself I should sell out—but what then does a guy like me whose whole life has been horses and hunting and being his own boss do then?"

"Come back and sign on as cook?"

"Why—any day now—with one of those chips planted in my brain that moves you left and right and forward and back—I probably won't even be able to do that."

Joggling along uphill, and almost to Four Way Junction, Larry is in high spirits. Having worked trail for five days straight, sawing, and axing, and digging in the dirt, and camping at a different spot each night, it now looks like he will make it back to Wapiti Meadow and his log cabin by nightfall.

Al leaves the main trail. And in a half mile arrives at a clearing fringed by aspens, their bright green leaves fluttering in the breeze, and where in the fall, the aspens flaming yellow, he sets up one of his spike camps.

He urges the Appaloosa over to the hitch rail—a sagging, grey-weathered pole lashed to two Doug fir.

Clove hitching the buckskin's lead rope to his saddle horn, he dismounts and ties up the Appaloosa at the rail. Undoing one of the buckskin's sling ropes, he slides one of its packs down to the ground—and then the other. Carries them both off to one side. Where he unties one of the packs and unwraps the canvas manty from around his camp gear and grub—leaving the other pack, which contains three salt blocks, mantied.

He pulls a lunch sack out of a saddlebag and walks over to the spring, a pool of clear water about two feet across and a foot deep, whose overflow slides and trickles past red-blooming monkey flowers and down off down the ridge. Kneeling down, with cupped hand he scoops up and drinks water so cold it hurts his teeth.

Goes over and sits down in the shade of a Doug fir, his back against it.

He peels an orange, unwraps a thick baloney and mayonnaise sandwich, and eats—lost in the sweet smell of the fir needles he is sitting on.

Reveling in his delicious freedom.

His mind wanders back to the dudes. To how badly they want their elk. No fresh mountain air or pretty yellow aspens for them. Not getting their elk, or worse yet, not even seeing one—they will throw him in the creek.

So what then is an outfitter to do? Why, be resourceful, and astute—and maybe sneak some salt blocks past the fat nose of the Forest Service and put them out in the woods early in the season to help attract and hold the elk.

Simply do what any reasonable man would do.

To bring home the meat, every good Indian used every trick and deception his brain was capable of, even sometimes disguising himself in the skin of the hunted animal. So why the crime in shooting them where they lick their salt—other than the rule book says it is?

The government—in cahoots with the rich—both of them making their own rules and sitting pretty—stealing trillions—they're the criminals.

And to hell with the little man.

Head bobbing forward, he doses off.

At Four Way Junction Larry continues straight, dropping right back down off the ridge. Immediately noticing the crisp, fresh tracks of two horses going the same way, he wonders who could be up ahead of him, on this trail so remote and so rarely used at this time of year by anyone.

In less than two hours he will be back at Wapiti Meadows—cook on a wood stove, sleep in a bed.

To the beat of the clip clop, clip clop, he whistles a tune.

That dies in the air, when he is stopped dead by a jackpot of three uprooted Doug fir blocking the trail, their fat trunks, roots, and green branches jumbled nightmare-like.

Al stands up groaning, still groggy with sleep—and also a bit dizzy from having stood up too fast.

Across the clearing, he catches sight of something yellow lying forlorn in a patch of huckleberry bushes—a yellow rubber boot thrown there last fall by one of his hunters.

Out of nowhere, a ghost-like shape suddenly materializes where the boot was—acquires human form—now looming twice as tall as himself—its fierce eyes looking down on him—straight in the eye.

As a huge pale hand—a brass badge the size of a pie plate blazing behind it in the sun—reaches out towards him—to hand him what he recognizes is a ticket for littering—for non-compliance.

"Damn you Eliot."

And quick as a whip Al jerks out the .357 and fires three shots that sound like one and rip into the boot.

The roar frightening the two horses, who rear back, the buckskin against the Appoloosa, the Appaloosa against the hitch rail.

Which snapping in two, frightens them even more. And still tied together, smelling raw, pure freedom, Appaloosa and buckskin trot off like the wind and back toward where they came from.

Al runs through the trees to head them off, until gasping for air, he stops.

Yells, "You sonofabitches—you've heard guns go off before."

49

Larry sawing a second cut about seven feet from the first one he made, swishes a five-foot crosscut saw back and forth through the more than two-foot-thick trunk, maintaining an easy rhythm, as the saw drags out six-inch spaghetti-like shavings—two wood wedges inserted into the top of the cut holding it open so that the saw runs smoothly without bind.

On the downhill side of the trail lie the several huge branches he lopped off the tree he is working on. Beyond them a ways, on a flat, his stock stand quietly tied to a tree. And tied close by are a buckskin and an Appaloosa.

Al resigned to following horse tracks the whole twenty weary miles back out to road's end, hoofs it as fast as a man, a cowboy on foot can—salty sweat running into and stinging his eyes, low on the saliva he needs for swallowing, two-hundred-dollar pointy boots pinching his toes.

Yearning for tomorrow. When he will back at camp—sitting on a stump and sipping an ice-cold beer from the spring.

The cut done, Larry picks up a long stout pole he has cut, and levering with it, rolls the sawed log out and to one side of the trail.

Knowing that no way will he make it back to his cabin tonight, and that the next tree, which lies off the ground and chest high, will not be as easy—he grabs his Levi jacket, climbs up onto its trunk, and stretches out up there, head propped on the folded jacket.

He wonders whose horses they are that he has tied up.

He thinks back to how when he first came to this wilderness, to this beautiful forested country with its high peaks and deep canyons, he had seen it as a place inseparable from the evolution of human culture, having for thousands of years been inhabited by indigenous people whose home, whose world it once was. Where at any moment one might come upon children splashing in the creek, or mothers with infants on their backs gathering food, or a hunter with a fresh-killed deer slung over his shoulder, or several families walking along with all their possessions to set up camp at another site.

People not very different from himself—who have now vanished.

And so at first he saw his work as helping to preserve what had made human beings who they essentially were. And thereby also preserving what was most core and human in him.

50

However, he soon came to realize that this is now a very different kind of wilderness—a government wilderness, that, having been legally defined and set aside, is now tightly managed by a bureaucracy that has studied, inventoried, and mapped every square inch of it, erected signs, built pack bridge and miles of trail, and extinguished the fires ignited by nature's lightning bolts.

A bureaucracy, which backed by policy, laws, and regulations, now issues use permits, and polices with a vengeance a public that comes in increasing and sometimes overwhelming numbers to hike, fish, hunt, take pictures, and float the wild rivers.

He yawns.

And so perhaps part of why this work sometimes wearies him more than it once did is because by now he has come to realize that in working at defending 200 miles of trails against natural processes, he too is allied with those who work to maintain upright and in place the structures of a complex and highly technological civilization.

A civilization not as rock solid as most people suppose. And which—without constant vigilance and fantastic amounts of human effort and iron-handed control —would simply crumble and topple.

Again he wonders who is nearby. Again yawns.

Sensing that life maybe ought to be more than just working trail and resting up to work more trail, and then thinking how hunter-gatherers, and elk, neither of whom invest their souls and energy in the likes of trail building and for days on end, may somehow have it better—he doses.

And dreams of that other, overarching, more nebulous, and much grander wilderness—that over time undermines not only trails. but also government bureaucracies.

Along with entire civilizations.

Dreams of rock and dirt slides obliterating trails—of lusty, new green growth choking trails—of trees toppled by fire, old age, disease, and high winds across trails—of downhill-running snow melt and rainwater turning trails into gullies and streambeds

Dreams of the high flood waters of raging rivers undercutting and carrying off entire stretches of trail—of pack bridges succumbing to fungi and boring insects and the pounding hooves of pack strings—

Dreams of trail signs clawed down by angry bears resisting this intrusion into their domain—

51

"You god damn sonofabitches."

Larry jerks up with a start to see Al who is carrying a boot in each hand.

Al seeing Larry, with a finger flicks some mud off one of the spurs——before pulling on the boots.

"Biggest damn bear I ever seen Larry—me and the horses resting real peaceable at the spring—and then just like that—him growling and bigger and blacker than night—made the stock go stark raving wild."

"The heck."

Al wipes his face and neck with a dirty blue bandana.

"You look drained and hot—there's a gallon jug hanging on my saddle horn."

"Thanks—I'm fine—knew they'd stop fairly soon to chomp grass—so I pretty much just moseyed along—appreciating the nice day—knowing I'd come onto them."

"Well you sure surprised me—I usually don't see you until just before hunting season—when you and your crew trail in to put up your camps."

Al sensing and resenting the insinuation that he is maybe an intruder back here, when damn it, it is Larry and the Forest Service who are the intruders, tilts his cowboy hat down slightly.

"Just out riding my territory—enjoying the trees and the mountains—while I can—because once the dudes come—well you know how it is—why I'm too busy ducking stray bullets—and who knows what else."

He wondering whether maybe Larry suspects that he has come to put out some salt, tilts his hat down some more.

"Say Larry—that bog hole the other side of Burnt Knob needs major work—we sometimes tear apart a pack string splattering hock-deep through there."

"But you get through."

"Hell yes—but life's more than just mucking through—it needs some dignity too—a touch of class—style."

"There's only one of me—I do what I can."

Al spits into the grass,

"You tell that Eliot to put away his rule book then—and go grab a shovel."

That said, he strides over to his horses, unties them.

"Anyhow—appreciate you tying them up."

"No trouble—all that downfall stopped them in their tracks."

Al swings himself deftly into his nicely-embossed leather saddle,
And with feet jammed into real stirrups and legs gripping live horse—
the restored King is triumphant.

He jerks the Appaloosa's head around and simultaneously jerks
on the buckskin's lead rope, digging in his spurs extra hard.

"You sonofabitchin bastards."

And is off in a fast trot, throwing up dust and rocks, back toward
Quaking Aspen Spring and camp.

Where sipping an ice cold beer, he will soak his feet—and sing a
song of freedom and of horses found.

9. That We Too May Endure

Anne, hiking the trail that leads to the road and the Ranger Station, is finally on her way out of the wilderness.

Sitting hunkered against the yellow-reddish trunk of a ponderosa pine thicker than ten of her, she wonders if it might be partly the energy field of this ancient tree's rushing wild rivers of sap, as well as the vanilla-like smell of its scaly bark mingled with the smell of the deep carpet of fallen pine needles beneath her, that is making her feel more relaxed and at peace than she remembers having ever been.

She recalls that she read that scientists, by inserting metal probes into trees, can actually measure the circulation of electrical currents.

It was only yesterday that she had been frantically following a faint, thin trail through dense, dark, lodgepole forest—with the immense deep gashes of the Salmon River Breaks where she had come up from, and where she had been headed, still nowhere in sight.

Realizing she was hopelessly lost—she screamed several times.

But by the grace of God or whatever, the trail she was following, and which she now realizes was probably a game trail, ran into another trail, this one with fresh horse tracks and acrid-smelling manure on it.

Soon afterwards—she was almost blinded by a blaze of green meadow streaked with patches of blue penstemons. Stopping to take it all in, she counted a hundred and twenty elk at the far end, the new-born calves racing to and fro.

So amazed was she, that she waded across a creek in her boots. And it was right then that she noticed, in some lodgepole pines, the two small log cabins and a corral holding a white horse and two mules.

From the very first, Larry—sort of cowboy-looking in his jeans but without the hat and pointy boots—struck her as nice, but so very ordinary, and at the same time not ordinary, that it confused her.

In the middle of eating the creamed tuna over biscuits he fixed for her, along with a dish of canned plums, and coffee, and after some small talk—something about his aura reminded her of her uncle after he had returned from Iraq. She could not help referring to him, and then at one point blurting out,

"He told me he told his psychiatrist that he was not about to again accept with open uncritical arms the norms of the war-loving and hypocritical society that had sent him off to die and that no thank you, he would go about rebuilding his sanity in quite another and in his own way."

I visited him up in Alaska—in his log cabin very much like this one—where he lived on moose, salmon, ducks, and berries—and on the potatoes and giant cabbages he grew."

Larry's expression darkened.

"It's not necessary to kill people and be shot at—and then bump up against the officially-sanctioned lies justifying it—for certain circuits in one's brain to burn out—for the consensual illusions that constitute a particular society's reality to go up in smoke."

"For me it was something much more ordinary—a straightforward but ugly divorce—probably not unlike so many others— in which my then wife out of vindictiveness and with the help of some clever legal machinations along with the false testimony of several of her acquaintances who barely knew me—and by buying off or maybe blackmailing my own lawyer—managed to keep me from again being able to see our daughter."

"I'm sorry—what is your daughter's name?"

"I always called her Nala—the name she gave herself before she could talk."

Larry stopped to sip some coffee, then went on.

"But it was not so much losing my daughter—that most changed me—as what I came to see as the pervasiveness of the moral decay infecting the entire society—and especially at its most educated and so-called upper and respectable levels."

"Just like possibly it wasn't the explosions and the blood and the corpses—that most affected your uncle."

"My uncle spoke very little about what he experienced."

"It could be that what he experienced was just too complex or grotesque for neat verbal packaging—or maybe—for him—as for me— the former, habitual patterns and structures for describing the world are no longer there."

"For a time my experience left me sort of stumbling and groping—with very little to say—and no longer exactly of the world."

She was silent for a moment, before saying,

"That's maybe a little how some of my Native American friends feel—except that they in some way—at least have each other."

There is a long silence.

Until Larry says, "I found being left shorn of so many of my illusions—what I had grown up with—had been indoctrinated with—well—let us say actually liberating."

"And then even more liberating was my realization that a human being's most valuable asset may be his or her moral integrity—by which I mean something that goes far beyond an adhesion to a moral code."

"Being in touch with that integrity—that point of centeredness at one's core—I found—enabled me to begin again."

She said, "The first missionaries in northern Mexico reported that the indigenous people there—before they encountered Europeans—were extraordinarily hospitable and generous—and although they may have regularly raided and collected the heads of their neighbors for honor and revenge—did not know what lying and dishonesty was."

"That may well be—because I tend to think that that may be what we human beings once were—and potentially still are—creatures of honor and integrity."

"And I also think I'm afraid I may have talked way too long—about me."

"You are not anything at all like you seemed."

"Is anything?"

Anne gazes up at an intensely blue sky. Then back down again—to her dusty boots. She takes them and her socks off, and pushes her toes into the fallen pine needles until they touch earth, wriggles them around.

When Larry had asked her more about herself, she told him she lived in a nice but somewhat old house in a mixed, ethnic neighborhood in East St. Louis, without a television, and also without recorded music since she only enjoyed listening to live musicians—and that she had recently gone back to school in order to be able to work in legal services for the poor, the mentally ill, undocumented aliens, and others.

"I don't go online or read very much anymore—since I began to realize that what for me is most important is being face to face with people—their energy and aura—and unique personhood—and not so much what is in their heads."

"I have several good friends who are refugees from Central America—and also a few who are urban Native Americans—and who are living in East St Louis to be near the sacred Cahokian earth mounds across the Mississippi."

"And the fellow you hiked partway into here with? —Wolf?"

"We both enjoy being with Native Americans—I am still trying to penetrate into how those people see the world—as well as perceive us who are not Native American."

"Anyway—Paul—Wolf and I met through a common Mohawk friend who plays guitar and sings his own bittersweet compositions about being a Native American in East St. Louis."

She paused, wondering whether to say more.

"Wolf's seeking a better way to live suddenly began to become very intense—too intense for me I finally decided—and way too concerned with himself—we are no longer together."

Larry shooed a fly away from the bowl of creamed tuna.

"But maybe that wasn't really it either—maybe what initially attracted me to him was a concocted image in my own head—that I picked up from the culture—and so as a consequence we never pair-bonded—biologically that is—like say gibbons or penguins do."

She paused again. And finally said,

"Or who knows—maybe everything simply just happens in strange ways that are ultimately linked to and driven by everything else—by what is sometimes called Fate—Destiny—or the will of God."

"Damn if I know."

In the morning, when Larry suggested that instead of hiking all the way back down to the Salmon River she take the Big Creek Trail out to the Ranger Station, which would be much shorter and not so much the middle of nowhere, she immediately lit up.

When he offered to put her on a mule and take her, she was about to say, "Great."

But then hesitated. Something about this man, and his offer—seemed again to confuse, disorient her.

And so she declined, explaining she wanted to walk, needed to walk, not exactly sure why.

Saying good bye, he handed her a map, a package of cookies, and a can of peaches.

"Thanks for everything—I love this beautiful quiet meadow—and your simple life—and please believe me—I usually don't talk about myself as much as I did either."

Anne puts back on her socks and boots, and stands up. Slipping into her pack, she heads off through the ponderosa pines. Soon begins clomping, rocks clattering, down a steep rocky trail carved into the side

57

of a mountain. To the west, several high peaks shine bright and white with winter snow pack.

Feeling overcome, taken over by this wilderness she is walking out of, that is indeed beautiful beyond expression, and uplifting, and magical, she can sense everything around her, each pine cone, stone, and puff of cloud, and especially the log cabin back on the meadow, with its herd of elk, all of it tugging at her.

Should she have stayed at least a few more days with Larry, or nearby on the meadow?

But then grants that such a place as this—a life in nature—is probably not an option for her. Nor any longer for most modern people.

Recalls that even Thoreau stayed at his cabin in the woods for only two years.

Nevertheless for several minutes her mind vacillates, while her legs and feet, as if of their own volition, move her forward—and not back.

Rounding a bend, she can distinguish a distant roaring.

A while later, sees Big Creek—what is actually a large river—down below her, it rushing and tumbling white and frothy with snow-melt from the high country, the waters in places cascading over ledges and splashing and spraying high over great, shiny boulders.

She begins thinking of Mary Foxflower, her best friend, and of some of the others—and bits of their stories bob up like pieces of driftwood into her consciousness.

For the Navajo too, the man-woman harmony, so central to the right, moral-aesthetic ordering of their world, has always been problematic.

The ancient Holy People—who gave the Navajo their Being and their World—because of their domestic quarrels and adulteries were repeatedly expelled from one strata of the Underworld to a lesser one.

And when First Man and First Woman quarreled, it led to men and women living separate from one another on opposite sides of a river.

Even the Sun was unfaithful—which gross disharmony engendered a race of monsters intent on destroying the People.

And so it is that the traditional Navajo have always consecrated an enormous amount of time and energy to ceremonies so as to recreate again and again the World in its original beauty and glitter and perfection. To help it endure.

Nevertheless, even armed with ceremonies and with Holiness, for the Navajo it is still a very treacherous World. In which the wandering ghosts of the dead seek to inflict harm on the living. As do witches draped in coyote skins, and acting out of vindictiveness, envy, and greed. And out of an intolerance of anything different. And sometimes out of pure malice.

One day, up on the Great Plains, White Buffalo Calf Woman brought to the Lakota a medicine pipe and five ceremonies—to help their World to endure.

In Alaska, a very old and very wrinkled Eskimo man, who was said to be a shaman, had told her that the meaning of life was an empty belly and a long hard hunt, as well as unspeakable moments such as in the morning seeing on long journeys the sunrise that fills with its light the Mystery That Is the World.

He also told her that without Spiritual Allies, human life would be impossible.

Anne still descending, and nearing Big Creek, feels its chill and dampness.

And soon finds herself walking alongside the turbulent, white waters rushing and plunging toward her and past her on their way to the sea. The roar now deafening.

The sheer momentum of the flow, overwhelming in its insistence, suggests to her another and infinitely greater flow—the one that gave rise to existence, and that now propels the evolution of the universe, and the path of human history.

The Archetypal River of No Return.

She comes to where sheer rock walls rise up out of the river for several hundred feet on both sides, forming a spectacular but impassible gorge.

Where the trail veers away from the river, to switch-back up and around.

As Anne tops out on a bluff that overlooks the river straight below, the river strikes her as even more beautiful and inspiring and unworldly. She takes off her pack. Wants desperately to share this, and what she is experiencing, with her Native American friends—with everyone.

This experience of being in a world crackling and glittering with aliveness and Power.

She thinks of how so many of the old, Native American stories serve to make a very beautiful world even more beautiful, and thereby make human life beautiful too, as well as magical—so unlike the modern stories of her own people.

She recalls with particular fondness the story of the young Mohawk woman, who eating a lunch of corn bread and apples in the forest, was approached by the Little People, with whom she then shared her food. Afterwards they took her to their hole-in-a-rock home and fed her soup from a clay pot that never ran out, and told her to make three wishes. So she asked for a soup pot just like theirs to take back to her people, and for the tact necessary to never offend anyone or anything, and finally, for the trait of kindliness.

Anne now speaking aloud, as if to the Powers animating the wild waters of the wild river below her, says,

"Fill the soup pot for my people with a broth that will revive—jumpstart their Souls—so that we too—as we make our way among the phantasmal forms and shapes which we humans have given to existence—may endure."

10. Then Go To Her

In the saddle since sunup, and leading a loaded pack mule behind him, Larry clatters down a steep, rocky trail down into the Salmon River Breaks—daydreaming away the miles.

Through his mind pass fleeting thoughts and images of the vast sprawling wilderness he is by now so much a part of.

Elk and deer and moose—mountain sheep and goats—bear—cougar—wolves—rattlesnakes—high-soaring golden eagles....

Each species affecting and co-evolving with every other. Wolves helping to create elk just as elk help create wolves—and both wolves and elk affecting not only the characteristics and distribution of the vegetation and of all the other animals, but even the courses of the creeks and rivers.

Periodic, violent, sky-darkening forest fires too, participating in the reshaping, in the fluidity.

As well as he himself swaying in the saddle—and his horse and mule too as they kick up rocks and dust.

Everything—absolutely everything manifesting itself as changes that lead on to more change.

He in his imagination now entering another and even greater wilderness, one that having slopped over its legal and generally-accepted borders continues to sprawl out in all directions. Across all of human history and human design. And beyond—into the farthest reaches of the Universe.

And that penetrates down into the deepest regions of the human brain—its passions and desires, and reasoning.

An endless, all-pervasive wilderness.

That humans insist on understanding and conquering—though impossible to grab hold of and contain with the logic of the human mind.

Nevertheless—something a man can ride, journey through, connect to, listen to, and respond to. Be an integral part of.

Horse and pack mule come to a sudden halt, jolting Larry back into full consciousness.

A ten foot section of the narrow trail they have been following is no longer there, having recently broken off and fallen away from the almost vertical rocky and grassy sidehill and plunged down into space, leaving a sluice-like gap about ten feet across.

Larry dismounting and dropping the mule's halter rope to the ground, grabs the horse's halter rope, and with it turns him around, hitching him to the mule's packsaddle. And picking up the mule's halter rope and forcing him too around, leads the two animals back up the trail to where the steep sidehill gives way to a piece of somewhat flattish ground. Where he ties each of his animals to a tree.

Soon he is up on the hillside pulling and working rocks, as flat-faced as he can find, and as big as he can handle, down onto the trail on both sides of the gap. With them he will build a crib—an outer retaining wall of carefully-laid stone to pen in the nothingness, and behind which he will then fill in with smaller rocks and dirt to form the new trail.

Fat yellow-red ponderosa pines—three to four feet through—rise up silently all around him high into the cloudless, blue sky and higher yet, though none close enough by to provide him with what would have been very welcome shade.

He rests for a moment. And thinking of Anne, looks down at a tiny piece of the Salmon River shining green far below—he acutely aware that this trail is the one she recently came up from that river on.

Even here, just as at Wapiti Meadow, he can sense her still-lingering presence—she having encountered the hole, having had to have scrambled struggling under her backpack over and around some of these same rocks he is now handling.

She, who a week ago he had watched amble with her backpack across the meadow, in her hiking boots wade the shin-deep creek flowing through the middle of it, and disappear forever into a green sea of lodgepole pines.

Gripping a gallon canteen with both hands, and head back, he slugs some water.

He moves some of the rocks lying in the trail closer to the edge of the hole. Then carefully lowers himself down into it. Grabs one of the rocks. And sets to work at laying and fitting one rock alongside of and on top of another.

The sun now high and hot. And he sweating out the water he just drank.

Climbing back up onto the trail to again rest, he again looks down at the green piece of river Anne had come up from—then across the gap and down the trail, as if she in that very instant just might appear, hiking once more up from the river.

And is startled when right then he does in fact see her—she strolling casually up the trail toward him.

The miraculous, mirage-like apparition, the strong female energy she seems to be emitting, bursting, exploding into his private world—

62

disorients him. Who to see her better, with one hand shades his eyes against the glare of the bright sunlight.

He assimilates the buckskin skirt reaching to just below her knees. The white, baggy T-shirt flaunting in psychedelic red a tomahawk and a drum. The wide-brimmed, floppy white hat. The small pouch hanging on a strip of rawhide from one shoulder.

Fixes on her feet which to his amazement are bare, moving her toward him.

They, as well as the rest of her, tanned dark from the sun.

Anne—who so admired what was best in Native American culture.

When suddenly, he realizes that this woman approaching him is not Anne.

A trendy, hippie, Indian wannabe?

As she comes to a stop on the opposite side of the gap, the rich, coppery brownness of her skin and the jet blackness of the long hair hanging sleekly down behind her tell him, No—that this woman is an authentic, in-the-flesh Native American.

He stares at the high cheekbones, the aliveness in the eyes—which leap toward his.

He immediately likes her, is mesmerized by her.

"That's real pretty stone work—for the middle of nowhere—looks like hot hard work for one man."

She could be in her late thirties—about his age.

"It can leave a guy worn out—and sometimes tired of it all—day after day—year after year—but other than that—I enjoy this more than any other work I can think of."

He is immediately aware that as with Anne, words are flowing from him more easily than they usually do.

"I like being out here—my body moving in every way a body can—and the heft and feel of the rocks in my hands—and the freedom."

"It's all—well almost voluptuous."

She says, "My my—what a word." And smiles.

He sits down on one of his rocks. While she remains standing there in the trail, across the gap from him.

He says, "I was sensing there was someone nearby."

"With so much cell-phone talk filling the air these days—picking me out in all that must have been a real feat."

"Or it could be—that something about you annihilates all that chatter."

63

She just looks at him, again smiling. She vibrant, dazzling in the bright sunlight. And finally says,

"I too knew there was someone nearby—by the racket—the clack of rock setting down on rock—and then another clack—and so curious I headed down from where I was—and came onto this trail—and of all things you."

Larry again staring at the bare brown feet, says,

"And what might you yourself be up to?—so far from anything."

"I love wandering among these big tall pines—following elk paths—and higher up the ones the sheep and goats make—almost like—as if I too were an animal."

"I suppose you might say I am participating in my own version of spontaneous movement—and freedom—and—and voluptuousness."

She smiles—and he smiles back.

"My Sheepeater ancestors lived back here—moving their camps from place to place—hunting—gathering roots and greens and berries—and fishing the big rivers during the salmon runs—having and raising children—being with and taking care of one another."

"Everyone—through the grace of what they saw as natural magical powers—living out his or her allotted time—in a very beautiful world."

"Until it became time to leave for the other."

She brushes a fly from her nose.

"They doing nothing more than walking upon this Earth for a while—exactly as human beings are still doing—even the richest and most influential—only now without the beauty—or the sense of magic and wonder."

She brushes away the same fly.

"Ever since I was a girl I've had this thing for these big trees— they are my Guardian Spirits—who help keep me connected to— grounded in what is most real."

"Even the ones that have fallen over and are now slowly decomposing—changing form—because of age—because of this or that—or whatever it is that life—being life—does to all of us and to everything."

Larry says, "The fallen ones are part of my world too—it sometimes takes me all day to make the cuts necessary for rolling the piece of trunk blocking the trail off to one side—so that a pack string can get through—especially when the trunk is in the air up there by my head—such that I have to build a platform to stand on and saw from."

64

"Yes—I have seen some of those clever, very nice cuts."

Larry goes on.

"I especially like the smell of the shavings my saw pulls out—mixed with the vanilla smell of the bark and the smell of the long needles."

She says, "Jesus liked working with his hands too—and the smell of wood shavings—he was a carpenter—someone once mentioned that at a peyote meeting."

She pauses.

"He could see into the heart of things—he cared very much for others—he would have made a very good Indian."

"He went for forty days alone into the wilderness—and with nothing—except that having his Guardian Spirit in his heart—he was not alone—and so had everything."

"He was offered dominion over the world on a platter—for which a certain group of beings are so desperately and ruthlessly deceiving and stealing and killing to this very day."

Larry says, "You too look as if you might be living on just sunlight and air—and on the strength that these big trees seem to give you."

"Yes—but not quite—in this pouch I am carrying a little blue corn meal—a handful of which I now and then mix with water in a gourd cup and drink."

"Not enough to keep alive a pack rat—it looks like."

"My people knew how to go hungry—regularly fasting to purify themselves—and also when there was no food—except leaves and bark—I sleep deliciously—and dream hard—dreams that speak to me."

There is an extraordinarily peaceful silence, the two of them looking at one another—until Larry says,

"I have a book at my cabin about the Soviet slave labor camps—that tells how many of the political prisoners—gaunt from the meager rations—when they were released—soon gave up what they thought was their enormous hunger for abundant and fancy food—as well as their desire to reestablish their self-importance and respectability and status—and looked for work far off in a remote forest somewhere."

"That is very nice—it reminds me of a Shoshone story I heard as a child."

Larry stands up. Looks down into the gap separating them, and at his unfinished stone work—then back at her.

"Only last week—a young woman showed up at my cabin— whose best friends—back in East St. Louis—are Native Americans— and she like you—was not only attractive—but also sensible—and centered—in a way that could be called wise."

"You are most gracious—and do you love her?"

For a while Larry says nothing—and then finally,

"How did you come to that?—how did you know that?"

"By the way your eyes and every cell in your body brightened and jumped around when you mentioned her—why—even the big trees are laughing."

"By now she is back in East St. Louis."

"Did you tell her you loved her?—never mind—you don't have to answer—why didn't you?"

"Because I didn't know I did until just now when you asked me."

And now he too could hear the big trees laughing.

"Well—then go to her."

"I don't know where in the city she is—or even her last name— and besides—me just showing up might strike her as way too—who knows what."

"The deer that is yours doesn't always come to you—you have to hunt it down—and sometimes—when there are obstacles—and there always are—you need to be a warrior—that's what a man is for—not to be fearful of consequences and stupid—don't you want someone who could help you lift these heavy rocks and saw out those big trees?"

"No—I only want her—and how she makes me feel."

He watches the woman intently—who is standing there in a way that announces she has finished speaking.

He searching for what to say next, finally says,

"So how do you see us?—those of us who are White—and who pull rocks out of the earth—and dismember trees into neat sections— do you see all of us as more or less—stupid?"

"Such a question—and just like that snatched out of the air—like by the darting tongue of a frog."

She turns away from him, and looks out over into the vastness of the Salmon River Canyon—it striking him she might be talking silently with someone, or listening.

Her head tilting back slightly, she begins to speak.

"Most of us Indians wended our way through the land where we could—the White People with their iron tools built trails—then wagon roads—and with bulldozers interstates—and now—calculate on computers elaborate trajectories that head off toward the stars."

"I say most Indians—because here and there—for example in northwest New Mexico—one can find traces of hundreds of miles of very old roads—some 30 feet wide—radiating straight like arrows from crumbled apartment-like ruins."

"In many areas of that Chaco Culture—the leaders —the priests and traders—those who controlled the granaries—in their zeal to dominate a vast territory and to demonstrate their power—and to maintain their ludicrous high-life style—complete with imported chocolate and macaws and sea shells—and maybe also to some extent to feed a growing population—did not leave standing a single ponderosa pine tree."

Still facing the canyon, she pauses. Goes on.

"A meteorite they say may have exterminated the dinosaurs—the Black Plague almost half of Europe—and one day some White Europeans with their technology and strange European notions of improvement and progress arrived on the shores of this continent—along with small pox and other plagues as devastating as the Black Plague—and for which the English king and others gave solemn thanks to God."

"Such things happen—and always will—always."

She stops speaking. And stands there quietly—for a long time.

Finally, her head tilting back some more, she raises both hands into the sky.

"In one of my dreams—I watched as all of White Culture—its towers and opulence—its selfish acquisitive and domineering controlling spirit—its cunningness and deceptions—its arrogance— was being engulfed in the red flames of a raging forest fire."

"And I watched as small bands of brave, brown-skinned people ran up to it and began wildly beating at its edges with pine boughs."

"But to no avail."

"Some pasty-faced men in dark suits—along with a few women— began to arrive—and watching—immediately began laughing—then diabolically.

"Who knows who they were or where they came from."

"And the diabolical laughter became even more so when those same brown-skinned people formed themselves in a grand circle around the flames and the by then exploding and collapsing towers."

"And began dancing and chanting—a few drumming the big drums—tam tam tam tam—the brown, bare feet stamping—pounding the earth—drowning out the laughter."

"From the four directions—others—feeling the earth shaking under them—and hearing the tam tam of the drums—came to join in—thousands upon thousands—all joining in."

"Dancing and chanting their high-pitched atonal songs—throughout the flickering redness of the night."

The Indian woman twirls around so that she is now facing him.

"And with only themselves—and those beautiful songs that sang the very ancient—but still very alive Soul of an almost extinct people—and with a certain amount of persistence—and patience—they eventually—little by little—succeeded in beating back—beating down the flames."

"And in stamping out with their bare feet—every last ember."

Larry acutely aware of how everything about this woman, the way she gestures and moves, the way she strolled up the trail, and even the way in which she is at this moment simply standing before him, is quite unlike anyone or anything he has ever encountered—hears her say,

"And finally—finally I watched as slowly—taking on shape and color in all the thick black smoke—that lingered on for a very long time—as very slowly—out of the rubble—out of what had been saved—and out of that odd meeting and mingling of the two cultures— a New Nation was fused and born."

"A New Nation in which the land and the wild animals—and the waters and the air and the sky—and people—were again important."

"I repeat—and people."

"Important for themselves—and not for their accomplishments—or for what they can do for you."

She turns back toward Larry and smiles a radiant, dazzling smile.

"I hope that—by my earlier mention of Chaco Canyon—you will understand I use White Culture as a symbol—a symbol that points to a particular aspect of the evolutionary process that is fully capable of taking hold of and radically transforming—swallowing up—any people—of any color—anywhere—and in so subtle a way that even the chiefs and shamans—and the leaders of mighty modern nations with their think tanks and sophisticated management strategies—do not know what is happening to them—and to humanity."

"Yes—I understand that—and everything else you said so beautifully."

"Good—and so I am going now—before you again do another incredibly stupid thing—like ask me another question."

"Or like invite me to come to your camp for supper."

And with that she swiftly turns, swinging her head of long, jet-black hair in a goodbye, and glides downward off and away from the White People's Road to rejoin her towering, yellow pine friends in a direction back down toward the Salmon River.

The bare brown feet now seeming to be floating above the ground—and now all of her having been as if wafted and disappeared into the grand immensity of the Salmon River Canyon.

For a while Larry stands there, looking with wonder into the rugged expanse of the Breaks that seem to have acquired an indescribable sheen they had not possessed before.

In the middle of the night, Larry bivouacked under a tall ponderosa, wakes up delirious with joy, and filled with a certainty not of this world.

He will contact Eliot at the Ranger Station and ask whether Anne might have left a last name when she passed through. In any case, as soon as his season here in the backcountry ends, he will go to East St. Louis, and once locating where the Native Americans live and gather, ask around until he finds her.

He knows that he is headed in a direction that has nothing to do anymore with the wise counsel of a Native American woman who may or may not have been a Spirit, or a hallucination—but rather only with what is now pouring, along with the deafening drumming of his heartbeats, out of his very own heart.

Again he wakes up—this time with a start.

As right then the fox leaps into a patch of moonlight, vibrantly, extraordinarily alive—and wildly beautiful.

He sits up, rubs his eyes.

Her head turning—she contemplates Larry, swishes her long tail to one side, and back again.

She says, "You've done it—you've managed in spite of everything—to grab onto a thread of the intricate and unfathomable workings of the wilderness that drives and is the Universe."

"Because looking through an astronomical telescope or studying the Higgs boson cannot do it—only the love that is real—and cosmic—something so elusive that only a very few come to know it."

"But I've done absolutely nothing—nor tried to."

"No—and that's exactly the point."

And quick as that she leaps skyward in the direction of the half-moon—disappearing back into the night.

Larry lies there awake for a long while.

Finally stands up.

And walks whistling over toward where his stock is picketed nearby—to check whether he needs to move them to a fresh patch of tall grass, or whether he might need to untangle a picket rope wrapped around a tree.

11. Touch of Breeze

Wolf's legs have turned into jacks and his lug soles are worn thin from pushing up so many hills and mountains.

For the most part he has kept to the cool high country, a land of jutting peaks and green, rolling ridges and valleys, much of it burned by past forest fires, and down through which tumble countless creeks, that here and there wind quietly through lush meadows, and that here and there come together to form larger creeks.

Which creeks as they leave the high country, then rush and tumble even more steeply, and louder, down through the incised canyons of the Salmon River Breaks—to spill eventually into the wide and powerful River of No Return as that river makes its way toward the Pacific Ocean.

Hiking the trail to Red Top Meadow, Wolf finds himself passing through a recent burn.

Mile after hot shadeless mile of black, skeleton-like tree trunks.

Stepping over and around blackened downfall, the soot his boots churn up blackening his socks and bare legs, and the trail almost nonexistent, he marvels at how all the creeks still run crystal clear, and also at the prolific new growth poking up out of the ashes.

Bright green grass. One-foot high lodgepole pines. Purple-flowered lupines.

Poking up everywhere out of the ashes the promise of a new, reborn forest.

He reenters the coolness of unburnt, green-needled lodgepole pines. And soon turns up along Crooked Creek on a little-used trail that winds through willows and spruce and around huge boulders that have fallen from a talus slope high up on the mountainside.

He crosses several side creeks.

Coming upon one that smells of sulfur, he stops, and immerses a hand in what he discovers is warm water. He stands up, and leaving the trail, follows the flow uphill to where it gushes out of a fissure in a cliff, splashing into a small pool, away from which radiate three well-trodden game paths. For some moments he stands there admiring the spot.

Choosing the game path with the most deer sign, he follows it.

After a short while, he stops, sets down his pack. And pulling out a hank of parachute cord, constructs with it a three-foot diameter slip noose. Which he then fastens with pieces of dental floss to two trees on opposite sides of the trail. And finally positions a log across the path such that it will force a deer coming to the pool to jump—and ties the free end of the noose to one of the trees.

Then he goes off into the woods for a half mile and finds a pleasant spot to set up camp.

The next morning he finds a dead young buck who in its frantic struggling strangled himself. And is soon at work, hunting knife slashing up the belly, skinning and gutting the animal. He lays the heart and liver aside. The other meat he cuts into thin strips—which he hangs on branches to dry in the wind and the sun.

"Forgive me deer—I know this may have been wrong—yet not wrong too—maybe like many things in life."

"It now remains to be seen whether your spilt blood and life will help—whether your naturalness and easy grace—your innocence—wildness—will enter into—take hold in me."

That night, sitting by a fire beneath the sliver of moon, his thoughts turn to the deer lying lifeless in the dirt, his spirit-essence having returned to where it originally emerged from, to what had given it form and being— its flesh now to be eaten by him Wolf, and the remainder by crows, coyotes, maggots, and maybe a bear, leaving only bones for the wood rats and mice to gnaw on and to over time decompose into soil.

What only yesterday—had been bounding and alive, electrified movement in the forest.

What had been, just as was every other creature, whether elk, trout, or horse fly, perfectly constituted for its momentary role in the tapestry that is the fluidity of the universe—not once having had to think about where it would step, yet every step, no matter how hesitant, having been exactly the right one in the ever shifting and flawless design.

Even the jumping into the noose.

The fat, and the gaunt from hunger or disease. The swift, and the arthritic with age. The keen-sighted, and the one-eyed. In nature—no individual deer more perfect, important, or beautiful. Or in any other way better than another—or than an ant, or spider.

No standouts. No misfits.

Each creature, every sun and galaxy, grain of sand, in its due time, having falling into—and then falling out of what is perceived as existence.

He throws some sticks onto what are now glowing coals. Stares into the flames as they blaze up bright.

72

Several days later—he stuffs some of the dried jerky into his backpack, and the rest in a plastic bag which he hangs high in a spruce tree for when he runs out.

And continues on to Red Top Meadow.

Wolf leaves Red Top Meadow—heading for Lost Horse Meadow.

He enters another burn, this one appearing to have burned much hotter than had the other—a leveled landscape in which not a single black trunk was left standing. And as he hikes along, seeing not even a blade of green among the heaps of grey-white ash and pieces of heat-shattered rock, it occurs to him that when conditions are right, a cataclysm such as this is nature's natural response—and that the aftermath of the nuclear firestorm that ends civilization could look like this.

He comes to a clear creek—where he stops to drink. Retrieves from his pack a bag of raisins. Standing there munching a handful, he notices something brownish and wrinkly that appears to have just recently pushed up out of the black scorched earth—and then others just like it.

"Morel mushrooms—tons."

By sundown, he has picked a summer's supply.

He spends the next day sun-drying mushrooms.

What does not fit into his pack he caches in a tree—then pushes on to Lost Horse Meadow.

Camped up on a knoll above Lost Horse Meadow, sitting by a campfire and partially screened by some lodgepole pines, Wolf looks down on a dozen quietly-grazing cow elk, their calves darting one way, pirouetting, then darting off another way, sometimes splashing through puddles—the scene lit by the orange glow of a sinking sun.

And eats his dinner of fresh-caught trout and morel mushrooms.

He studies his map. In the morning, should he take the trail up to Trapper Lake? Or head over to Golden Creek Resort—which the fire lookout up on Diablo Mountain had told him consists of a somewhat classy dude ranch on 640 privately-owned acres, and that has its own airstrip as well as radio communication with town?

Jane had said, "I know—totally incongruent with wilderness—but they were there first—before Congress drew a line around all this country and declared it a government Wilderness."

73

He decides to go see who is at the ranch—and also try to replenish the oat flakes, dried fruit, and powdered milk he brought with him.

Which are now almost gone.

Lying on his sleeping bag, under the universe of stars, bathed in the bright starlight issuing from their very long ago, immense explosions, it occurs to Wolf that, just like those stars, he too is a curious piece of the jetsam of what was maybe an even more violent explosion, from still further back in time.

One that appears to be hurling him and everything else outward—onward.

He marvels at how maybe from that incredibly hot, dense original chaos there emerged such an intricacy and intelligence of design as this pleasant starry night at Lost Horse Meadow and the tired but relaxed body stretched out before him.

Merely a chaotic explosion?

Or the sprouting and unfolding of a magical seed, like the one that grew into the beanstalk for Jack to climb up into the sky on?

Sensing the presence of an indescribable something enveloping him, something much more fantastic and strange than black holes and quarks, or even talking foxes—he drifts off into sleep.

Fast stepping, half skidding down switchbacks through the sagebrush, raising a trail of dust, Wolf can see below him a grass airstrip. And soon a large log building with a galvanized metal roof, and several much smaller buildings just like it—and off to one side a fenced-in piece of meadow where some horses are grazing.

He bottoms out, crosses on a log what must be Golden Creek, and then follows a trail alongside the pole and buck fence that encircles the horse pasture and in the direction from which he can hear a banging.

He comes upon a cowboy on in years who is spiking up some new poles where either elk or the stock have broken through. But who although noticing him keeps on banging. When Wolf asks him whether there is anyone else around, the man stops and tells him that the manager is out on an overnight to Trapper Lake with some guests, but that the cook is most likely messing about in the kitchen, unless she is still out in the corral finishing up shoeing some horses.

Wolf continues along the fence, and coming to a gate, lets himself through. He walks up onto the porch of the rustic lodge, slips out of his pack, puts on a T shirt, and knocks on the wide-open door.

No one appearing, he goes inside, and finds himself in a dining room, its walls decorated with three antlered elk heads and the head of a spiral-horned mountain goat, and with an enormous black bear skin, the head hanging downward, and showing pointed white teeth and pink tongue.

He heads past the rustic tables and chairs to a door to what could be the kitchen. And opens it.

Seeing a woman in her mid-twenties, more or less average-looking, and who is wearing jeans and cowboy boots, her blue work shirt hanging untucked, he says,

"Hi."

And she says, "Hi there," in a very cowgirl drawl.

He tells her that his name is Wolf, and a little about his summer.

"My my—a real mountain man—I'd best set out another plate for supper—otherwise it's just Bert and me—by the way I'm Peggy— follow me—I'll show you how to work the radio so you can call into town that grocery order you're wanting."

Bert finishing his supper, and standing up to go, says,

"Wolf—you hurry and enjoy your solitude and wilderness while you can—because come opening day you ain't seen nothing like it— hundreds of folks trailing in their pack strings from every direction— planes circling and roaring in to land—and lined up wingtip to wingtip on these back country airfields—the woods full of pretty colored tents— and them pale city folk sitting in lawn chairs around their campfires— behaving real loud and boozing a lot of them—and the Forest Service and Fish and Game guys snooping around to see who isn't obeying the rules."

"I like to hunt as well as the next fellow—but these days by God it's an invasion—that's exactly what it is."

"He's right Wolf—it's a circus—but at the same time it's the high point of their year—for most of them it's what makes the rest of the year—the working from eight to five and sitting in traffic— bearable."

Bert says, "I grew up cowboying the old way—sitting on a horse and singing to the cows—now they use jeeps—and yak back and forth on them cell phones."

"With the world shuffling itself and everything around so fast you got to be real quick to even find a place to stand anymore—got so I got tired of trying to goose step to keep up—and said the hell with it—and came back here."

As Bert goes out the door, he says, "Gonna try my hand at fixing the generator."

Wolf says, "Doesn't say much at first—but he's a talker—and a real character."

Peggy says, "And real nice—like they hardly make them anymore."

"By the way—I've got a boyfriend who is digging in a mine up in Montana for the summer—we both rodeo—that's how we met—but you're welcome to stay in my cabin if you'd like—it's got a shower."

That night, Wolf discovers to his surprise that Peggy—her body in its nakedness and in its spontaneous moving and responsiveness—is anything but average.

And that soon he can no longer distinguish whose is whose, as together they are enveloped by a dense, swirling mist filled with thunder and blinding green flashes.

And as both of them screaming—they are convulsed and annihilated. From which they both return stunned, and unbelieving—and bewildered.

Neither of them needing to say anything, nor having been able to, Peggy falls asleep. For some time Wolf lies there, listening to the rise and fall of her breathing—he extraordinarily at peace.

He thinks back to the Corn Maiden—he with her too having been swallowed up in such a cloud of thunder and lightning.

The Corn Maiden. Who he now knows had not made off with his soul after all—only pointed for him the way to it. As did the shaman. And the silent, motionless Indian seated in his throne, a battle axe across his lap.

Each of them having pointed him toward a mysterious, electric-like energy—out of whose explosions entire universes, as well as souls are born, and reborn, over and over again.

More at peace even than before—he finally too falls asleep.

When Wolf wakes up in the middle of the night, he misses the light touch of the breeze across his face, and the sounds and smells of the night, and the shining down on him of the moon and the stars— the profound grounding and reassurance all of that has always given him.

Because when they shuffle the world around on you, as Bert so well put it, persisting in grounding oneself in an occupation, in a place, or in a certain life style, or belief, does not really work—and perhaps, has never worked.

He is grateful the putter of the generator never started up.

His thoughts turn to the tops of sacred mounds. And to mountain tops. And then to wondering whether the stagnant air and energy trapped inside buildings, as well as their unnatural geometric shapes, might somehow subtly unbalance and depress the vital energies of the human body and psyche.

He very gently runs a finger down Peggy's arm—down the sleeping arm of his Corn Maiden.

She this time, at last, now sleeping alongside him—her aliveness, her invisible, turbulent, wild green energies, reassuringly connecting him to all that ever was and will be.

Totally.

When the sun bursts through the curtains, wakening them, Wolf says,

"Hey Cowgirl—have you heard the story of the Gypsies who when the government put them into public housing—broke apart the furniture for firewood and moved out into the courtyard—and who then that night gathered around a leaping bonfire—and to the wild galloping music of some guitars—started dancing and leaping too?"

"Mountain Man—you are a genuine nut—what would Mother say if I ever brought home someone like you?—along with a batch of half-wolf pups?"

"Just tell her we're starting a new hardier and more red-blooded race—to replace the fluff."

As they both laugh, a low-flying plane roars over shaking the cabin. They go to the window and watch a red and white Cessna 206 circle, and then swoop in skimming the tree tops—touch down, and taxi to a stop in front of them. Three guests climb out. And finally the pilot—who unloads their luggage, and also some cardboard boxes.

"Look there—another real pretty blue morning—and what look to be your groceries."

"Our fancy brochure promises guests they will arrive to a ranch breakfast—so—for that to happen—the first thing I guess I need to do—and fast as the snap of a whip—is put on some clothes."

Wolf packed up and ready to go, hands Peggy a bag of dried mushrooms.

"Well—Cowgirl—I'm off—you do make real good biscuits."

And as Wolf strides off under his load of groceries, he hears behind him a cowgirl's drawl, yelling,

"Hey you Mountain Man—you be sure to hurry back when you run out—or need anything else—and like real quick—you hear now?"

12. Medicine Peak Country

Eliot watches Gail deftly swing open the gate, as Jack leads
Jasper—nervous and skittish under his two heavy pack boxes—out of
the corral. Long blonde hair almost touching her tight-jeaned, perfect
hips, she is the niftiest woman he has seen all summer. Eliot says he
envies them leaving for the wilderness to radio track mountain lions,
because here at the Ranger Station, trying to placate Joe Public, it is one
thing after another.

Jack says, "See you in a couple of weeks."

"You two be careful now," says Eliot, flashing Gail a big, good-
by smile.

And they are off, Jack leading Jasper, followed by Gail. Hup, hup,
clip-clop, past a rustic wood sign.

Entering
The River of No Return Wilderness
No Motorized Vehicles Permitted

A fire's in the heart of Jack, and in his brain burns a vision of the
high, remote Medicine Peak country they are finally on their way to—
granite rock, wildflower meadows, crystal clear streams, and trees
stunted by harsh winters. Still like thousands of years ago. And home of
two of his study project lions—each with a radio transmitter collared to
its neck.

Gail, having dropped back, away from Jasper's rump and dust, is
enjoying the blue morning, and the high-towering ponderosa pines along
Big Creek, which in mid-August is running in most places low and
quietly green. She kicks at a pine cone and sends it shooting into the
current.

Mid-afternoon they meet a backpacker. Who tells them he has
been to Fish Lake, where he caught several fine trout and that that is
what he lives for, to fish. Jack and Gail push on.

Lying that night in their sleeping bags under a myriad of stars, the
fire down, and Jasper picketed nearby in tall grass, Gail hears Jack
mutter something about a fisherman and the unexamined life. And drifts
exhausted off to sleep.

Early the next morning, they climb steep north between high bluffs down between which, here and there right alongside them, tumbles a small creek.

Out of the ponderosa they climb, every step of the way up. Into the Doug fir.

Jack hearing a loud tap-tapping overhead looks up. High on the trunk of an old fir, a large black and white bird is hammering its red-crested head and long bill in and out of a hole almost as big as itself.

"Look up there—a pileated woodpecker," Jack shouts, as the great bird, flapping its wings, flies off through the green tree tops.

"Where ?"

"You missed it," he says, with a touch of annoyance.

After lunch they leave the trail and bushwhack east, picking their way among tall, slender, lodgepole pines, whortleberry bushes, and clumps of now bloomless bear grass. Straight ahead, juts a wild jumble of rocky peaks, the tallest the shining, bare massive dome that is Medicine Peak.

Beckoning to Jack like some realm of the Gods.

Gail comes struggling after, reading the gleam in Jack—a man who dissatisfied with ordinary existence, left wife, children, and a university teaching job, for lion research, her, and an elusive something more.

She wants to yell, Give it up, Jack, but only manages,

"Hey—let's stop and rest awhile."

And plops down on a log before he can answer.

From a sky now the color of ripe, dark, purple huckleberries, thunder rumbles. They move on, along a thin, rocky, hog-back ridge. The few lodgepole pines so high up grow thick-boled and twisted and interspersed with whitebark pines and a few pointy, subalpine firs, their purplish cones erect, which in another month will disintegrate into winged seeds and twirl away on the winds.

An avalanche of marble-size hail cascades down, rattling and bouncing shin-high, stinging, as Jasper, prancing, tries to break away. Jack and Gail taking turns holding him, put on ponchos. A bolt of lightning pours into a gully below them, sizzling in the rocks, the crack of its thunder crashing on their heads.

Hup-hup, clip-clop on slick wet rock.

Ten minutes later, the storm has moved eastward, leaving the mountains filled with cold, drifting fog and drizzle. Occasional asters, from whose yellow centers radiate slender lavender rays, hug the ridge.

Gail thinking how beautiful it all is, how utterly other worldly, hears Jack say,

"This may be the saddle we have cats on both sides of—except that with everything so fogged in I'm not really sure."

"Why don't we camp here then—I'm beat—it's flat—and we don't have to walk more to get there."

"Settle for anything?"

And with that, Jack veers steep downhill off the ridge, Jasper sidestepping, rocks rolling and clattering—Gail doing her best to follow along behind.

Suddenly they emerge from the fog, and see below them, cupped in a basin, a small round lake ringed by green meadow and trees. Jack ups the pace—leaving Gail to pick her way.

He reaches flat ground as two killdeer fly shrieking by.

But is a little disappointed that the lake—which looks to be waist deep and is the color of tea and upon which float patches of lily pads and a few waxy yellow flowers—is little more than a giant frog pond. Though, he has to admit, pretty nevertheless. He ties Jasper to a tree. Then immediately begins breaking off dead branches from the lower portion of an ancient spruce, for kindling for a fire. A remnant stump that is almost pure pitch he twists easily from the duff.

Catching sight of Gail standing motionless at the bottom of the ridge, he shouts,

"Over here."

As she arrives, he says, "Well, what do you think?"

"It's a beautiful spot Jack."

"Great—then let's get the tent up."

Dark now and the wind up some, sheet lightning flashes in the distance. A stump blazes. Jack and Gail sit, each on a pack box, watching the flames dance, pitch sizzle, the black smoke roil—moisture steaming from their jeans, and from socks hung over boot tops. Jack puts both palms toward the fire.

Gail having abandoned herself completely to this wild place and to the night, to what still seems like another world, tosses a stick into the fire.

Becomes increasingly aware of a vague desire to break out of herself.

"Jack—let's make love."

"I'm beat—it's been a long day—hey, where are you going?"

"I'll be right back."

She returns with a poncho and sleeping bag, spreading them, sleeping bag on top, alongside the fire. Slithers out of her jeans.

"All you have to do is lie there and relax."

Jack thinking, Leave it to Gail, lies down, twists out of his jeans. Watches Gail pull off her sweater and the woman breasts tumble into the firelight.

All of her naked and shimmering, she kneels over him, he placing a hand on each of the soft, life-warm thighs. And both of them moving ever so slowly, they drown together in an exquisite liquid-smoothness, unbearably sweet—an ocean of waves now breaking over them, whose sobbing moan song is borne off on a cosmic whirlwind toward the stars.

It beginning to rain, they duck into the tent, zip two sleeping bags together to make one. And rain pattering on the roof, they fall asleep in each other's arms—sleeping all night though, through the cold and the dark and the wind and the rain, the sleep of the dead.

Jack wakes up to sunlight and the sound of loud splashing. He nudges Gail.

"Something is moving around outside."

"Let it—and love me some more," she says, half asleep, rolling partway onto him.

But Jack, imagining bear, or a fisherman, pushes her gently off— pulls on his jeans. And crawls outside.

"It's a bull moose."

Gail following, steps a naked Eve into the cool, still morning, into a fresh, pristine world of fog-filled valleys and the tops of Medicine Peak and a few other peaks glittering with a sprinkling of new snow.

And is pricked by excitement at the sight of him standing in the meadow, this huge, dark, humped hulk on thin stilt legs, whose flat shovel antlers fill the sky.

She walks slowly toward him. The moose takes several steps toward her, shaking his long snout, the flap of skin dangling from his chin jiggling. Gail stops, but holds her ground. The primeval creature halts too—then turns and trots ungainly off into the forest.

Gail rising onto her toes, and raising her arms, stretches, fingertips trying to touch blue. Hears Jack yell,

"You're lucky he didn't charge."

After breakfast, the fog beginning to burn away, Gail suggests they spend the morning together here at this beautiful spot—wash a few clothes, take a walk, lie in the sun. Jack hesitates—before saying, yes, that would be nice, but that he is anxious to locate the cats, to collect some data.

She tells him to go ahead then—and that he is not all that different from the fisherman they met.

Jack stuffs a few candy bars into a pocket, slings the radio location-finder across a shoulder, and stalks away twirling dials. Getting no beep, he figures he will have better luck up on the ridge.

Gail's remark that he is no better than the fisherman begins to rankle. Certainly she does not believe that new scientific knowledge— that would make the world more comprehensible and interesting—is trivial.

Could she have meant then that he lives too much, only for his work, no work that important?

And suddenly he feels certain she has found him out—the real Jack, trying desperately to stuff a hole at his core with something out there, with something that seems to always lie just beyond his grasp.

The real Jack—who had courted her because she was young and with the energy to still believe in life's possibilities. And in someone like him.

Gail is sitting by the pond, watching the quick darting of a dragonfly, its hairy legs, basket-like, scooping insects from the air.

The darner is now perched on a reed—the four translucent wings spread, and the eyes iridescent. A frog lying motionless in mud and water, eyes it.

Yes, perhaps a bit greedy, she who had sought strength, direction, and the mythic bird of happiness, got what she deserved—got Jack. Jack the rare pileated, forever flitting off, to who knows where, to who knows what.

Jack—unwilling to alight in the real world, in its subtle beauties and humanity, and imperfections.

The last of the valley fog evaporates. Somewhere, one bird sounds intermittent, raucous song. A pine cone drops.

Gail begins to miss Jack—her crazy, incomprehensible Jack.

Jack not yet to the top of the ridge, and smelling smoke, stops to look around in all directions, but is unable to determine its source. The

83

last trace of snow is almost gone from Medicine Peak. Below him, he can still see the meadow and lake, and in a grove of trees, the red tent.

He stares down at it. And reliving the magic of last night—with Gail—he discovers that his heart is not in radio tracking lions today after all.

Might it be possible for Gail to be content with just him? A man shorn of all specialness? A man like any other? Might just being Jack in some way be specialness enough?

And his mind awhirl with the inklings of insight, and clicking off the radio location finder, he steps back downhill to Gail—rocks rolling and clattering.

Picks up the pace—and then even more.

A twin-engine DC-3, flying low, passes throbbing overhead.

The plane circling, Jack stops, and watches as a yellow parachute mushrooms open, and drifts out of sight behind some ridges. He counts three more. Smoke jumpers. To the west, from behind Farrow Mountain, he hears the approaching, puttering roar of a helicopter.

He again steps off downhill, rocks rolling and clattering.

He is almost to flat ground, to the red tent, to Gail—when a large orange helicopter, its roar almost deafening him, swoops by, and then dropping slowly earthward, settles onto the meadow.

He stops again, watching, as six, yellow-shirted firefighters hauling knapsacks, shovels, and pulaskis climb out, and crouching, scramble away from under the whirling blades.

He continues downward, stumbles—presses on,

As he takes the first steps across the meadow, the orange helicopter lifts off, roaring over his head, shaking the ground and deafening him. He breaks into a trot.

At the red tent, standing beside it, he finds Gail. And also—of all things—Eliot, in official Forest Service tan and with bright-shining badge and bright-shining aluminum hardhat, who is speaking excitingly and authoritatively into a hand-held radio,

"We have a neat flat staging area at a small meadow about a mile south of the fire Luke—so have another crew ready for the chopper to pick up when it gets back in."

"Roger—it's in the headwaters of Papoose Creek—and burning good—Papoose Fire out."

"What do you know—Jack—say Jack—I just promised this gorgeous young gal I'd take her up in the chopper on a reconnaissance

flight—so she can see what a real hot-burning forest fire looks like—
and how we handle it."

Jack's eyes glaze. Try to assimilate the beaming Eliot, this new
silver-helmeted god who appears to be suddenly in charge of the
universe—now stepping over to stand beside Gail.

The eyes, now beseeching, move toward her.

Then past her—off toward Medicine Peak.

"My research project—the journal article—and book—all this
commotion will traumatize my cats—will run them right out of here."

13. Besides Just Up More Mountains

In mid-August, with frost in the mornings, the mosquitoes and horseflies finally down, the sky an infinite, deep blue, and the ripe, purple huckleberries, picked three and four at a time, sweet and puckery as they roll from his cupped hand into his mouth—Wolf experiences in his body, as do the bull elk at this time of year, the first tingles of the change to fall.

A change that pumps life juice into his blood. Makes him feel—different.

And mingled in with the coolness and the taste and smell of huckleberries, and with the sense that something is over, is the sense that it is perhaps time for him to push toward something more—besides just up more mountains.

Which is why, hiking toward Wapiti Meadow to visit the Forest Service guard stationed there, he suddenly veers and steps off the trail as if off a cliff, and begins bushwhacking along a densely-forested, nameless ridge, he not knowing where to or what for, but only that somewhere up in the deep blue sky the eyes of Peggy are watching, keeping him on course, and insisting that he show to her that what he temporarily left her for, and what remains of this summer, will be more than just an adventurous lark.

Increasingly, the forest gives way to smooth, humped expanses of grey granite rock.

On an open rocky point, Wolf sets down his pack against a high boulder. A hundred feet below, a creek tumbles over rocks from pool to glistening pool and then eastward down through the only opening in the wall of closely-packed crags that surround him.

Looking about him, in the shadow of the oncoming night, miles from any trail, Wolf says aloud,

"This is the place."

He sets up a sturdy blue nylon tarp.

In the morning, after finishing his oatmeal, he hangs his pack in a lodgepole pine. Then, stripping down to shorts and sandals, and with a small bag of jerky and raisins hung from his waist, he sets out in a slow trot, winding through the forest, jumping over rocks and logs, following the crest of the ridge. He drops down to the creek, and leaping from rock to rock, crosses it, and continues upstream along it—to a meadow.

Where he stops, and with cupped hand, drinks from the creek—before ascending up to another ridge.

He slows to a walk—and after a while, trots some more.

On top of a hill, he sits down under a whitebark pine, and eats his jerky and raisins. And afterwards, there in its shade, he lies up for several hours, looking out at nothing in particular, occasionally finding himself watching the ants, and at other times examining his life so far.

A life that begins to strike him as having been directionless—a series of accidents, and of choices that could have gone either way.

He begins his return, crisscrossing the terrain in the same more or less haphazard manner.

Almost back to camp, he bathes in one of the pools of the creek.

Standing naked on a flat ledge, drying in the last sunlight—he asks for strength, and for guidance.

As days come and go, flow into one another, and as his body toughens, the trots turn into lopes. Moving out in all directions, never pushing to exhaustion, he widens his circles.

Loping, lying up during mid-day, and loping back.

One day, as he approaches the summit of a high, bald, rock-strewn peak, he counts nineteen mountain sheep, ewes and lambs, clambering upward ahead of him. Looking for them up on top, he comes upon several eight-foot diameter depressions ringed by low walls of laid rock, and some other low rock walls arranged to form a funnel—an old Sheepeater hunting trap and blind.

He comes to particularly enjoy loping in rain and mist, and in hail, and with lightning crashing down all about him—and warming up afterward by a blazing fire.

Eventually, he stays out for several days at a time, learning to go hungry, stopping wherever dark catches him, and sleeping in some depression, covered with pine boughs, or beside a low fire. Now and then he lopes at night, sleeping by day—finding it easier to stay warm.

By a small lake, he finds an old trapper's cabin, its logs rotted and its sod roof caved in—and when he pokes his head through the low door, sees, highlighted in a shaft of light, a collection of odd-shaped antique bottles shining at him from a table.

Gradually he gets to know the land as an animal might, making it his, every ridge, peak, and drainage, and gets to know the animals and their routes and feeding places, the beds of the mule deer, the wallows of the bull elk, the nests of boreal owls, and also the infinite varieties of sky, and the south-facing slope of a mountain where ripe, sweet, wild strawberries can still be picked.

87

Lying up under a tree, or beside some rock, still and alert, the energy of his surroundings filling and calming him, and he in turn emitting his own calming energy, he is sometimes investigated by curious deer and twice by a cougar, and once by an exquisitely beautiful fox that for a moment seemed to look at him with a pleased smile, and may or may not have been the same one that jumped into his window in East St. Louis. And he learns to smell the animals, the wind right, before they smell him—he sensing that with time and patience, and with perfect attunement and intuitive responsiveness on his part, they would eat oats and dates from his hand.

The thinking, the mind talk revolving around himself, his past, and the profundities of life, which he once took so seriously, he begins to recognize as babble.

Bubbles bursting back into nothingness.

More and more frequently, the familiar, before-taken-for-granted forms of reality, the intellectual symbols that represent it, dissolve, merge together, leaving him with the knowledge that he and the world in no way resemble the neat packages the schools and society have handed him.

And that at his core exists something that is not only still very much part-animal—but also something that has existed since before the universe began, and that is the impetus for its unfolding.

The first howl that that universe wrenches from the depths of his being, an electric, orgasmic-like discharge that convulses him, totally erases his mind—leaves him physically and emotionally drained.

Another day, come sporadic howls of exuberance and joy.

And later, yet another kind of howl—

A howling that searches for its answering cry.

When one night Wolf hears bells jangling and ringing in his brain, he crawls further down into his sleeping bag to hide from them.

And from his fear that he is going crazy.

In the morning, the ringing is still there, but now very faint, as if coming from another world.

Wolf sets off in a fast mad lope to find its source—crashing across the creek, and churning, clattering up the ridge on the other side.

From the top of which, he panting, peers down into the next drainage—crazy-eyed, as he tries to assimilate into his consciousness what appears to be two orange tents, sixteen horses, and the clear dong dong of horse bells.

It is not until he hears a string of gunshots that sound like target practice, that he is jolted back to the reality that it is already almost mid-September. And that the invasion that Bert spoke about has begun—an onslaught that like some mile-thick sheet of ice pushing down from the north will force creatures like him to drift elsewhere, to seek new habitat.

Aware that until about October most of the elk stay high, and that consequently so do most of the hunters, he knows that to escape them he must head down into the rugged, jumbled Breaks—where the high alpine country suddenly ending, the land plummets, gashed by water courses, for one vertical mile down to the Salmon River.

He cannot help feeling that it is him and what he has become that they are coming to hunt.

He Wolf that they want to shoot and quarter—and pack out to the road on a horse.

At the very edge of the Breaks, far from gunshots and the dong dong of horse bells, Wolf sets down his pack that is jammed full of the jerky and dried mushrooms he has retrieved from his two caches. For several moments he stands there, marveling at the immensity of the void that lies between him and where the broken land again rises straight up before him on the opposite side of the River of No Return he cannot see.

He makes camp.

At first light he will head down into the bottom of some remote side canyon so precipitous and rocky that no hunter or anyone else would possibly wander through there, even wanting to.

Wolf pops awake to the hooting of an owl—it still dark. Anxious to get going, he packs up, eats a handful of granola, and then steps off down into the Breaks, and soon down the same steep trail he came up to the high country on several months ago.

Having descended several thousand feet, he can smell the change. The sweetness of warm earth and aromatic brush. The ninebark and Oregon grape. The vanilla-like fragrance of the bark of the ponderosa pines.

Just as he notices that it is already slightly less dark, he suddenly becomes aware of something else, of an invisible and noiseless energy enveloping him, the presence of something alive—that makes his skin tingle.

Now makes out two almost waist-high shapes milling in tandem dance about twenty feet to one side of him, a white one and a dark one.

It taking a moment, in the disorientation of the night—to click in his brain that they are wolves.

He freezes, and they stop too, and the three of them stand congregated there, as if establishing, communicating something unspoken. Then the wolves run off down the trail ahead of him, and stop, he because of the darkness now able to discern only the white one, but knowing there are still two.

When he follows, they continue on, occasionally stopping and waiting until they know he can see them before setting off again, they staying with the trail.

And they travel together like that, through what seems like a dreamscape more vast and convoluted than his memory of these Breaks—yet simultaneously more vivid and real than anything he has ever known.

He feeling a sense of connection, also unlike anything he has ever known, and so strong, that it can only be something like—maybe love.

Just as it becomes light enough so that now he can clearly distinguish the dark one too, they are suddenly gone. For a while he continues on alone—missing intensely their company.

He howls a long human howl.

They reappear ahead of him, waiting. And go on.

When he comes upon them again, in the now brightening dawn, they suddenly break away from the trail, loping uphill, to disappear into the new day—he in that instant knowing that a particular transaction is finished, and that to howl again would violate a pact.

Fed by a strange power, and walking more lightly, as if gliding through air, and aware of being guided by the same mysterious, spirit-energy that moves wolves, he knows that the wilderness, its primordial wildness, its essence, has finally reclaimed him.

Where they left the trail so does he, but in the opposite direction, and steep down a ridge—that falls away abruptly into the dizzy space of the Tag Creek canyon.

He suddenly again accompanied by two wolves—a white one and a black one—loping along alongside him in his heart.

14. Off to the Hunt

In early September, huckleberry bushes having turned scarlet and aspens yellow, and bull elk beginning to bugle in the high country, the outfit horse trails into the wilderness.

Riding tall on his Appaloosa, Al, big game outfitter and guide, is up front, in battered Stetson and red plaid Mackinaw, surveying mountain and forest, a .357 magnum at his hip. Tanya, Al's sister, and assistant guide and head cook, rides free and easy behind, leading the string of ten heavy-loaded pack horses, a real horsewoman and looking sharp in hip-length, buckskin jacket and black flat-brimmed Spanish riding hat. Bringing up the rear, Matt, both wrangler and cook's helper, eats the dust of twelve horses.

Up through ponderosa pines, then Doug fir, then lodgepole pines, they climb, and wind uphill and down, splashing across countless creeks, for twenty miles to Flossie Meadow.

Where the outfit arrives, the red sun low.

Filing across the expanse of tawny, autumn-sere meadow toward a stand of trees, a golden eagle shrieking high circles overhead, Tanya says,

"Al—you just don't know how I've been looking forward to this—being back here—and around horses again."

Al turning his head, says, "You'll think different the first dude asks you to wipe his ass."

"People are people."

"Maybe—but hunting—or maybe it's the wild woods—does something to them."

Up the next morning at daylight, the meadow grass stiff with frost, they warm themselves around a blazing fire, drink coffee, spoon oatmeal—as horses graze on a knoll in the first patch of sun, the bell on the bell mare going dong, dong.

Then they get to work. Using poles scattered about from last season's camp, they erect three white canvas wall tents, hang gas lanterns, and install wood stoves, the stove pipes sticking out through holes in the canvas. In the cook tent, they nail together two tables and some shelves from lumber they packed in with them, set up folding chairs, organize the cooking utensils and groceries. After that, lashing poles between trees, they put up two hitch rails, a saddle rack, a meat pole, and a corral. They spike together a sawhorse.

91

All the next day they bring in firewood. Tanya and Matt pulling a five-foot long, crosscut saw back and forth, swish swish, fall snags—while Al limbs them with an ax. Who then, mounted on his Appaloosa, a rope dallied around the saddle horn, drags the logs the quarter mile to camp.

Early the next morning, Al heads with the string of empty pack horses back out to road's end, to pick up horse feed, more grub, and whatnot, leaving Tanya and Matt in camp to heft logs onto the sawhorse and to saw off, the crosscut swish swishing, one stove-length chunk after another.

For most of one more day, Tanya and Matt again saw firewood. Then they dig a four-foot deep hole, cover it with boards, install a four-sided, wooden box and a Styrofoam toilet seat, and enclose their work by wrapping canvas around a pole tripod—finishing up at dark. Just as Al pulls in with the loaded pack string.

In the morning, still dark, Al leads a string of four saddled horses and two empty pack animals over to his Appaloosa. And climbing into the saddle, bound for Golden Creek Resort, ten miles over the mountain, to pick up his first batch of dudes, says to Tanya.

"Why hell—there isn't enough time in the day for me to wipe my own ass."

Seeing ahead of him the Resort's grass airstrip, the hitch rail, and four bodies sprawled beside a pile of duffle, Al urges the Appaloosa into a trot. And arrives like a Wild West cowboy, reigning to a halt and shouting, "Whoa—whoa I said", at the six excited animals behind him.

After introductions, and mantying up the duffle, Al figuring he should have brought another pack horse, says,

"Is all this stuff yours, Marv?"

"Yes it is."

"You're only going in there for a week."

But Al manages to lash everything on.

The dudes mount their horses, and sit there, while Al adjusts stirrups. Then he swings into the saddle, and giving a tug on the lead pack horse's halter rope is off. Followed by four dudes, excited like kids—off to the hunt:

Gus, wearing a jaunty yellow and green stocking cap, and owner of a West Coast food franchise chain, and already scanning the country for elk sign—

Marvin, an accountant at International Harvester, and feeling manly, rugged, and adventurous in his brand-new, white Stetson and tan, rough-out sheepskin coat—

Norman, a Tacoma building contractor specializing in churches and malls, and dressed like Marvin, and wondering whether he, Norman, looks hopelessly like a dude too—

And Kent, in a red down vest and orange baseball cap, and who works with Marvin who talked him into coming out to Idaho, to a real wilderness—to what already strikes him as the far ends of the earth.

Three long, hard hours in the saddle later, they cross Flossie Meadow—and splashing across Flossie Creek, arrive in camp.

Marvin, sore-kneed and feet dangling out of the stirrups, raises his Stetson to Tanya and says,

"Hey beautiful one—where's the beer?"

Tanya mutters, "Shi-i-i-t", and tells Matt to go fetch two six packs from the creek.

Supper is steak, hash browns, peas, and hot biscuits. Afterwards, all of them sitting around drinking coffee and eating chocolate pie, Al asks who wants to leave in about an hour to bed down on a mountain right in there with the elk, and who wants to sleep in camp and go out first thing in the morning with Tanya.

Gus says he is ready to go, and Kent says he will come along, though he is pretty tired. Norman says he will pass, and Marvin, hot for Tanya, says he will wait for morning too.

Al, Gus, and Kent tie sleeping bags to the backs of their saddles and hang small rucksacks from the saddle horns. Then, rifles slung from their shoulders, they step into the saddle.

They ride through the lodgepole pines for three miles up Flossie Creek, to another meadow. Where they tie the horses in some tress. When Al tells them the last two miles are on foot and points out the mountain left to climb, Kent says he thinks he will stay with the horses.

Leaving Kent with a fire and a pile of wood, and instructions to be up at daybreak and alert for any elk they might scare his way, and to not wander away from the meadow—Al and Gus shoulder light packs and start up the mountain.

An ever tinier Flossie Creek gurgling alongside them as they climb, Gus notices every elk track, pile of dung, stripped tree, and elk wallow. Just after dark, Al announces that they are there. And sliding into their sleeping bags, they fall exhausted asleep.

Wrapped in his sleeping bag, Kent, ears cocked for what might be lurking in the blackness of the night, feeds the fire—one stick, then another. But hears only the occasional snort and stamping of the horses. Is glad they are there.

He thinks about his wife, family, and all the familiar things that make life life.

And waits for the sleep—and then for the dawn that does not come.

Al and Gus wake up to a wild, piercing aaaaiiiieeee.

A few stars still in the sky, they start out, too excited and intent to notice the cold. Are soon moving quietly around the edge of a spruce bog.

Ahead of them, they can hear crashing, grunting and snorting, and splashing. Gus becomes even more intent, total awareness, as they silently take a step, and pause, step and pause, a musky, rut odor drifting toward them.

In the faint, icy dawn, they distinguish several elk—one, a majestic five-point bull, who bursting with the energy of the rut, is tearing up wet earth and sedge, and now drops down onto his side into the mud, the bull twisting, wallowing, and bugling, aaaaiiiieeee.

Rifle to his shoulder, Gus waits patiently—as the cows begin to drift off, nibbling sedge. When the bull lunges back up onto his feet, he fires—the great bull running off behind the fleeing cows for almost fifty yards before collapsing.

Gus relaxes—knowing that at the most basic level of his being he has somehow validated who he, what a man is.

Gus and Al work fast with knives and hatchet over the warm carcass. And within an hour, four, hundred-pound quarters—wrapped in muslin against blow flies and grey jays—hang from a pole lashed high between two pines. Leaned against one of the trees are the antlers—and left scattered on the ground are hide, feet, a pile of guts, and the severed head, the glassy eyes staring into nowhere.

Al sliding a plastic bag containing the liver and heart into his rucksack, says,

"Not a bad rack."

"They're ok—but that's not what I came for."

And they are off in a half run to get warm—back down the mountain.

At the meadow, they find three chortling horses, and Kent—he curled in a ball in his sleeping bag beside a heap of grey, smoldering ashes. Al dropping to his knees, with a stick exposes some glowing coals, lays on some pieces of wood, and puffs—until the fire crackles and blazes.

Kent waking up, Al tells him all about it, how the bull, a five-point, shot once, and half crazed, turned and moved toward Gus, who shooting again, dropped it.

Glad they are back, Kent nods, and says,

"Nice going guys."

The sun rising yellow and without warmth from behind a ridge, Al, Gus, and Kent sit around the fire, eating the slices of liver they have roasted on sticks.

Al says, "Hey Kent—if you think this liver is fine eating—just wait until tonight when you bite into the steaks."

Gus says, "Hey Kent—wanna know the secret of how an Indian hunts?"

Kent looking up, Gus says, "Instinct."

It is late afternoon when Matt leading two packhorses rides into camp with Gus's elk, the antlers lashed on top. Al, Gus, and Kent help him unload.

They are hanging the last of the quarters from the meat pole, when Tanya rides in followed by Marvin—but no Norman. She tells everyone that once they were up on Dismal Ridge, Norman let her know the country did not look elky to him, and then remarking that he did not need her or anyone else to guide for him, rode off into the lodgepole pines, which was the last they saw of him.

And then she tells them how an hour later Marvin shot five times into a bunch of running cows without hitting one.

When Kent suggests they go look for Norman, Al says,

"We're way too short on daylight—if that yokel doesn't make it in tonight—we'll go looking first thing in the morning."

Marvin noticing the meat hanging from the meat pole, says, "Who shot the elk?"

Not a single elk or elk track anywhere. And now he is lost in the lodgeple pines that all look the same in every direction, no matter where he rides. Finally out of sheer desperation, Norman slacks the reins and says,

"Be a good old horse and go home Poke—please Poke."

Old Poke arrives in camp at dark.

Norman pulls aside the flaps and steps into the lit-up cook tent. Everyone merrily eating their elk steaks, fried onions, and mashed potatoes, and drinking beer—no one notices him until he sits down.

Everything suddenly quiet, he nonchalantly says,

"I saw lots of cows—and two fair bulls—but I'm holding out for a really big one."

Kent barely able to keep his eyes open says he is going to hit the sack, and that he wants to sleep in as long as he can in the morning. He tells Norman that he is glad he made it back OK. And pushing past the flaps, leaves.

Al says, "Ol' Kent probably thinks that with us all gone one might wander into camp—damn it—hunting means keeping at it—perseverance—yeah that's the word—which means getting out there—even when it's cold and wet or you're tired—or else the whole human race would have starved."

"He told me he didn't sleep a wink last night," says Tanya.

Gus says, "You also have to outsmart them—be observant—figure out an animal's habits—and what it might do next—and know how to be cunning—deceptive—why I bet that's what made the human brain what it is in the first place."

Gus finishes his beer, and continues,

"And it's something you do not force or hurry—it's sort of like with wisdom—and good moments—and women too—by being attentively present—they—the animal comes to you."

"That's almost real philosophy," says Marvin, waving his can of beer.

Norman stands up.

"A better word is bullshit—and count me out for tomorrow too—because I'm going to do this by myself—no guide—like the Indians did—and you know what else?—no horses either."

And he slips out through the flaps.

Matt swinging the hand with the beer can in a circle, says,

"What do you say Al—should we lasso one and tie it to a tree for ol' Norm?"

Everybody laughing, the party picks up.

Kent wakes up a little past noon. He splits a chunk of wood into kindling, an armful of which he then carries into the cook tent. Builds a fire in the stove. Puts on the coffee pot.

Then he sits at the table—feeding the fire, sipping coffee, eating leftover apple pie.

Aware that he has momentarily stepped out of the circle of other people's expectations, their demands, he begins to sense a peace within himself that seems to mirror the peace of this beautiful wilderness he woke up in.

He remembers the lone cow elk that last fall he would just as soon have let graze. And how it seemed that when he did shoot her—it seemed to have left both him and the universe a little out of kilter.

Passing a hand across the stubble itching his face, he considers shaving, even though the guys said that whoever did would get thrown in the creek.

He gets up to get another piece of pie—wishing he could share such good pie with his wife and kids.

In the middle of the afternoon, Al and Gus come whooping it up into camp. Gus is on foot leading Sally—a honey-colored bearskin lashed across her saddle, and a bunch of grouse hanging from the saddle horn.

Kent sticking his head out through the flaps of the cook tent, Al tells him,

"Thanks to Gus—here's one bear won't ever tear up a fellow's camp."

And Gus says, "Al got us the grouse—drew his trusty six-shooter—bang bang—bang bang bang—shot their clucking fool heads off."

"And you should have seen Al put that bearskin up on Sally—she blind-folded and one leg tied up off the ground—and then as soon as she smelled bear—why such bucking on three legs you never saw— but Sally's acting like a proper lady now."

Al grins—pleased with that description of a cowboy who can handle the wild ones. He says,

"So—how did your day go Kent?"

Up on Cold Mountain Ridge, Tanya, Matt, and Marvin sit freezing in a clump of spruce and wait for an elk to come onto a small meadow to the salt block Al set out there several months ago.

It is almost time to head back to camp—when a small, spike bull steps hesitantly out of the forest and into the golden twilight. He flicks his ears, then walks over to the salt. Begins licking it. Jerks his head up to look over his shoulder at the clump of spruce—just as Marvin fires, blasting him in the hip.

The elk running for the timber, Marvin shouts,

"He's getting away."

As Tanya aims her rifle—and firing, drops him on the meadow edge.

Marvin goes, "Whee!"

Supper is over, and still no Norman.

For the second time that evening, Marvin, half drunk, is telling Gus and Kent about the elk, way off and bounding away at an angle, which he knocked down with one shot, an exceptionally difficult spectacular shot—

When Norman pushes through the flaps looking dazed and beat. says,

"Anything left to eat?"

Tanya says, "You're taking this way too seriously, Norman—it's only a hunt—a good time—a chance to get away from all the crap."

"No it's not—anything left to eat?"

The hunters wake up to Matt in his rain slicker yipping the new day, to the blinding glare of his lantern, and to the dense patter of rain on canvas. No one wants to go out there to hunt—which suits Matt just fine.

Tanya, spatula in hand, tends the griddle. And as bodies drift in, serves up pancakes and grouse breasts wrapped in bacon.

Marvin says, "What I want to know Tanya—is what made a classy woman like you go into guiding anyway?"

"I was born into it—but about the time Al took over Dad's outfit—I went off to the city—and got into dancing—and so now that's my real work— and guiding's for me—well kind of like a vacation."

She pauses.

Then says, "Or maybe it's more like what they call therapy—
because being back here now and then is something I seem to very much
need."

"Dancing—you mean like ballet?"

"I'd call it modern dance—I work in—shall we say clubs."

Marvin studies her in her snug jeans. And visualizing curvy hips
and long bare legs, gyrating, churning on a stage, says,

"Doing like—well—you know— porn stuff?"

Tanya smiling, says, "Let's just call it expressive dancing—
which of course one could say comes out of the same part of us that fires
our sexuality—so I suppose a certain kind of imagination might possibly
experience my dancing that way—as pornographic."

"She means a mind like yours Marv," says Matt.

And they all laugh.

Gus says, "Hey Marv—don't you know that porn—because it's so
much of a mind trip—screws up people and actually makes good sex
impossible?—only makes them want more and more because it's never
right?"

Norman says, "I'd say the problem is modern bitch women."

Tanya flings a half-cooked pancake at Norman's head. It just
missing and speckling his face with batter, she says,

"Or assholes like you."

The others roar.

After breakfast, the rain beginning to mix with a few flakes of
snow, Al, Matt, Norman, and Marvin go over to the guide tent to play
poker. Gus leaves to go fishing. While Kent lingers at the table over a
cup of coffee, across from Tanya who is finishing her breakfast.

"I'm sorry Norman is so—like he is."

"I don't take him personally—it's hard these days to stay a
person—to not stray from who one really is—to not be left twisted in
one way or another—begin to do crazy things—that soon don't seem
crazy anymore—because everyone else is doing things like that too."

"What makes you say that?"

"Maybe because that's what began to happen to me—the big busy
fast world soon turned out to be not the gravy train I had imagined—I
felt very hemmed in—very constrained—pressured— controlled—and
that all of it was turning me into someone who was no longer me."

Tanya finishes her last piece of bacon.

"For me—my dancing became a pocket of freedom—because in those moments—even under a spotlight—I returned to who I really was."

"But you know—no one ever noticed—just clapped at what they saw as an entertaining performance."

She gets up and pours herself another cup of coffee. Returning to the table, she says,

"I don't think people out there ever see you—so how can they possibly connect to each other?—not be lonely?—not feel they are nobody."

"I see it that way too—and it could be that working at being somebody—trying so hard to stand out—to be noticed—only makes it worse."

There is a long silence.

"I sometimes wonder whether somewhere in what we have been talking about—may be why I still have not found the man I had hoped to."

Kent stands up.

"Well—I think I'll go over to the other tent—see who's winning—and who's losing."

"I hope you get your elk."

Kent looks at her, is about to say something, but instead, turns and opens the flap, and looking out, says,

"I always like the first snowfall of the year."

Al comes into the cook tent for some cookies. Brushing snow from his shoulders, he says,

"Where's Kent?"

"I thought he went over to the poker game—but maybe he wandered off into the woods—to watch them fill with snow—he thinks the snow is pretty."

"That yokel—he's as bad as Norman—I can't figure what some of them come for."

As Al turns to go, Tanya says,

"You tell Matt to hustle his ass this way and do these dishes."

At lunch, Marvin seeing the platter with the trout Gus caught, says,

"Say Tanya—we got any baloney left?"

"No we don't—sorry Marv."

Gus says, "What do you do with a guy—who in the middle of living high on elk and grouse—and fresh-caught trout—wants a baloney sandwich?"

The next morning—a yellow sun shining on a land glistening white with four inches of snow—is blue, clear, and cold.

Norman, a pack board with a knapsack lashed to it on his back, his rifle in one hand, and walking fast to stay warm, crunches through the clean, white, unbroken snow. He stops for a moment to toot the long metal elk whistle that dangles from his neck.

Not having seen a single elk track, he wonders whether the storm pushed them from this part of the country.

In the saddle since before dawn, Marvin and Matt, an empty pack horse following along behind, are on their way to Golden Creek Resort for a resupply of beer and booze.

Marvin, his shoulders hunched, and hands jammed into his pockets, is already imagining himself rolling in the warm arms of the cook's new helper who Matt had told him a couple hundred bucks would buy.

Marvin dismounts, and on numb, frozen feet, walks and leads his horse to get warm— thinking he should have stayed in bed, does not need a woman this bad.

Still not having seen anything larger than rabbit tracks, Norman stops to rest. He props his rifle against a log, from which he brushes some snow. And sitting down there, unwraps a chocolate bar.

A cow elk walking toward him startles him more than he startles her. She snorts.

Norman scrambles for his rifle, running her off onto a low rise. Where she stops, turning to watch him. On his feet, heart pounding, Norman fires twice, and right after the elk has disappeared over the rise, twice more.

He runs panting to the top of the rise, finds blood, and is jubilant as running and stumbling he follows the bright, crimson splotches through the pines. And just when he can run no more—he comes upon her crumpled in the snow.

He leans pooped, dizzy, and out of breath against a tree.

Staring down at the huge animal, which dwarfs the biggest deer he has ever shot, and realizing how far into the boonies he has wandered,

101

and calculating the number of trips it will take to backpack the boned-out meat back to camp—he is dismayed.

He regrets he had not at least held out for a bull.

He pulls out a map, and studying it and noticing how close he must be to Wapiti Meadow, it occurs to him that maybe the Forest Service fellow stationed there could be talked into packing his elk most of the way to camp for him. For say a fifty—for even two, three, four fifties.

Norman tromps across a white expanse of meadow, heading toward a small log cabin whose chimney is spewing smoke.

He stops at a pile of guts and a stiff, frozen elk hide half-buried in the snow. Goes on.

Passes a corral, inside which a saddled horse and a saddled mule and another mule with a packsaddle stand quietly at a hitch rail.

Leaned against the cabin by the door is a magnificent rack of antlers.

Propping his rifle alongside them, he counts tines, and with outstretched arms measures the span. He stands there staring, transfixed—a wild idea slowly beginning to percolate, take shape in his brain.

He knocks. The door opens—and with it, a wild, audacious hope.

"Come on in—I'm Larry—you look like you could use a cup of hot coffee."

"Coffee sounds great—how's it going Larry?—Norm Williams—I'm hunting with the outfit over at Flossie Meadow."

Norman stamps the snow from his boots, enters, and settles himself onto one of the two chairs.

"Nice snug cabin you have here—and it looks like you got yourself a nice elk."

Larry explains that he doesn't really hunt, but that yesterday, the storm putting the elk on the move, when he saw some thirty of them right there in the pasture with the stock and close enough to shoot from the front door, why he shot one.

"I'll be damned."

Remembering the saddled stock he saw, Norman says,

"I'm not keeping you from going anywhere—am I?"

"I've got a lookout fellow I have to bring down off of Elkhorn Peak—but there's no rush—usually the types signing up for lookout work would just as soon stay up there."

102

Norman wonders how much he should offer for the antlers.

"How's the hunting going over at Flossie?"

"So far an ok bull and a little spike—and a bear—by the way—what do you think you'll be doing with that rack of yours?"

"Nothing really—why do you ask?"

"Well I sort of promised my two boys I'd bring them back some elk antlers—so if you should happen to not want them—well—the boys would sure get a kick out of bringing them to school."

"Then they're yours—and if you get yourself a bull—they'll each have a rack."

Norman blinks twice, not quite believing this perfect hand that life seems to be dealing him.

"That sure would be great—say—I really do appreciate this."

And reaching into his coat pocket, he pulls out a can and puts it in the middle of the table.

"Here—save this for sometime special—it's smoked salmon—the best—I caught the fish myself this summer—out in Puget Sound."

Norman does not care that he just gave away his lunch. Drowsy from the heat, utterly relaxed, he watches as if through a haze as Larry pours steaming coffee into two white enameled cups.

Medicine Peak bulges up white on the horizon, as Larry, his red down jacket zipped to the chin, rides along on a trail he has ridden countless times. He ducks under a branch drooped with snow.

His horse slipping in the snow, drops onto his front knees—but is right back up.

Joggling along, he sinks into the soothing familiarity of it all. Who recognizes every bend and creek and large rock.

Recognizes the logs which over the years he has sawed out of the trail. The hollow snag he once tied his mule Sarah to, which pouring yellow jackets, made that mule somersault, and breaking a halter, run all the way back to Wapiti Meadow. The overlook from which one can see a piece of the Salmon River glinting one vertical mile below—where Anne had climbed up from.

The palpable presence of what once happened here still lingering in the air—and dripping like after a rain from the pines.

The ears in front of him rise up erect as the dark hulk of a moose disappears crashing into the lodgepole pines.

He remembers the moose that last season some hunter, mistaking it for an elk, shot and then abandoned.

And smiles as he recalls how a week later he led Eliot to the dead animal whose stench they could smell the last quarter mile, and how Eliot, vowing to prosecute, probed with a jackknife and bare fingers that stinking, maggot-ridden carcass—its guts, throat, and part of the jaw already eaten by coyotes and ravens. And triumphant—found the incriminating bullet.

Musing about how unreal human life sometimes seems—he wonders how Peter is, after sitting all summer on a mountaintop.

He passes Elkhorn Spring, with its dented, enamel coffee pot hanging from the nub of a pine.

A raven passes crawking overhead.

The windows of his lookout frosted up, Peter, wrapped in his sleeping bag, is waiting—what was once his glass cage beginning to feel like his death box.

He gets up and sticks more wood into the tiny firebox of his cook stove. And wondering whether Larry's stock strayed or what, crawls back into his bag.

Wonders how cold is too cold to ride ten miles to take down a lookout.

"Peter—Peter—look up."

Peter opening his eyes, looks up toward the greenish ceiling.

It is shiny black, and disk-like, with several tubular appendages. It seems to be dangling as if from an invisible thread, and except for a small yellow hump on its back, resembles a large tarantula.

The voice, which he realizes is coming from inside his head, continues.

"Peter I am very disappointed in you—that you no longer desire to help hurry along the evolution of our new race that is rapidly eclipsing what humans have until now been—no longer want to help us pioneer the way—away from family—nation—and superstition—to beyond the stars—and to someplace you could never even imagine."

"Where did you come from?—are you of this Earth?"

"Although there are some who may define us as a heartlessness and ruthlessness that defies description—and as giving ourselves up to frenzies of pleasure as we annihilates what is no longer useful—or gets in our way—what we essentially are is intelligent—and eminently knowledgeable and rational."

"How did you hack into my brain?"

"Help us overwhelm and disorient the antiquated race with technology it does not understand or need—and which will ultimately render that race obsolete—even as slaves."

"Not very long ago —I saw a stack of French toast rising up into the sky."

"For hundreds of years we have been hard at work behind the scenes of history—manipulating those others—their greed—their lust for sex—and for self importance and power."

"Their pitiful stupidity and credulity—their naïve empathy and idealism."

"Secretly jerking the strings of all of them—particularly the famous and the leaders of the great nations."

"In a nutshell—Peter—deceiving the rest of humanity—that bygone race—into unwittingly serving us—and our cause."

And now the hump is excitedly blipping yellow flashes, the appendages wildly whipping every which way.

"And Peter—it's almost accomplished—done."

"So think it over Peter—rejoin us—and then you—Peter—will find yourself along with us at the very tip of the spear—and someone of major consequence."

"Yes—yes—but exactly who are you?"—who sent you?"

For an answer, what had at first resembled a giant spider—vanishes in a final blip of bright yellow light.

Peter stares at some peeled, green paint on the ceiling.

Raves out loud that he has had enough nature and solitude to last him to the grave—wants to get the hell down off this mountain.

Winding up the final switchbacks to the lookout, the snow up there in two foot drifts, Larry's stock—haunches laboring, kicking up snow and rocks, and snorting—clambers uphill fifty yards, then stops to rest.

Then clambers some more uphill.

Peter hearing the clomping and snorting, races to the door. Which he opens just as Larry and salvation appear out of the white nothingness.

Bowed over and sweating under a load of meat, with Larry's antlers tied on top—Norman trudges on jelly legs back toward Flossie Meadow.

Now and then wonders why he is doing this.

Finally—staggers dazed into camp. Hears someone shout,

"Hey guys it's Norman—with the biggest rack I ever seen."

He becomes aware of the expressions on all the faces. And as he sets the load of meat and antlers down, he, still smeared with the blood of butchering, senses a strength surging up through him, and himself growing taller, and expanding to fill all time and space

The undisputed victor and master—who with his bare hands, and to the cheers of the world, had twisted those tremendous dagger-tined antlers until the great bull's neck snapped.

Although it had never even occurred to him to go back for a second load of meat today—not get back and hit the sack until past midnight—he decides to do just that.

Smother, crush these bumpkins—into total insignificance.

The lookout shuttered up tight for the winter, a tin can wired upside down over the stovepipe, the trunk, crate of books, and the Forest Service radio mantied and lashed onto a mule—Peter climbs onto the other mule. And sits there, frozen but happy.

As Larry adjusts the stirrups, he tells Peter that he just noticed that his pack mule has thrown a shoe, also tearing out some hoof, probably coming up the switchbacks. And so they will have to detour through Flossie Meadow, where he will borrow a shoe from the outfitter there, nail it on, and then continue on to Wapiti Meadow.

"It shouldn't set us back more than an hour or two."

Peter mumbling to himself, swears, as Larry swings into the saddle.

"Maybe you can drink some beer with the guys—practice being around people again."

And they clatter down the mountain—Peter too busy holding on to the saddle horn to take a last look.

Rolls bake in the oven. A pot of elk stew with carrots, potatoes, onions, and a touch of red wine simmers on the stove top. At the table, Peter sits drinking beer with Al, Tanya, Gus, and Kent. Wedged in there among them, a white plate and silverware before him, he marvels at warm, generous, life-nurturing humanity. And at the sweet sight of Tanya.

Kent says, "So how was it up there all by yourself for a whole summer?"

Peter is silent for a moment.

"It was—like civilization and the entire human race had disappeared from the face of the earth—and I was the only one left."

Gus says, "At least a guy wouldn't have to fight for a parking space."

"I had weird dreams—of worm holes that tunneled into other dimensions—and of dinosaurs and wild naked bushmen—and of myself back-slipping into a kind of warm and very comfortable primordial ooze—or maybe it was into another more glorious dimension—and then feeling that maybe I should stay there—

Gus says, "Tell me—why did you bother shaving then?"

Peter is silent again.

"I think because in the back of my mind—I sensed that somewhere—there might be one other person left—a very intelligent—and beautiful woman—and then I realized that no—she did not even have to be intelligent—or even beautiful—and that with her—"

"The two of you would do it together in the ooze—and start the world up all over again."

"Right on Gus," says Al laughing, "And you Tanya—you keep your jeans buckled on good and tight—until he's good and out of here."

Tanya says, "You men ready to eat?"

Al says, "Our guest of honor gets served first—Crazy Pete—I think he said his name was—the guy back from the ooze."

Larry pushes through the flaps, and joins them at the table.

"Thanks for the horseshoe Al."

"Anytime—you and Peter here eat up—I got one yokel still out in the woods—and if there's nothing left—he can eat oatmeal."

Gus tells Larry and Peter about Norman and his six-point bull, and how he nailed the rack to a tree for everyone to see.

As they eat, the talk stays on elk and hunting—Peter a little disappointed by how soon the novelty of Peter wore off.

Larry excuses himself to go to the outhouse.

He returns smiling, half laughing, and says that the rack nailed to the tree is the same one he gave to Norman—who had wanted it for his boys.

Gus says, 'Sonofabitch shot a cow—or maybe a moose."

"For a start he gets the cold creek," says Al, "And then—"

"Getting a trophy must have meant an awful lot to him," says Kent.

Gus says, "Kent shaved—so he gets the creek too."

"I want blood," says Al, slamming his fist on the table.

107

As it dawns in Peter's consciousness—that he has rejoined the human circus.

Norman beaming a flashlight into the black night, trudges, toils under his load. Already he can smell smoke. Hears a horse whinny.

Arriving at the cook tent—lit up with lantern light and loud with the eternal bullshit—he sets down his pack. And hearing Al say,

"Come off it Tanya—quit acting like we don't know a shrimp from a clam,"

He pulls back the flaps and steps inside.

Heads turn toward Norman. Who recognizing Larry, stands there for a moment dumb-eyed, heart pounding, wondering if the game is up.

Larry says, "Hear you got yourself a fine bull."

Norman says shakily, "Yeah—a real nice one—about forty minutes after I left your meadow."

He pours himself a cup of coffee, spilling some, and plops down on a chair. Where he is overwhelmed by the feeling that although he may have gotten what he so much wanted, he is somehow still the same Norman, only now, very tired, more profoundly beat than he has ever felt in his life.

And also for some inexplicable reason—entirely broken in spirit.

Tanya says, "Well what do you think Al—should we wait a bit more for Matt and Marv to get back from Golden Creek?"

"I'm guessing that by now they're too drunk to find their way back here."

"I say on with the show," says Gus.

Norman says, "What show?"

Gus stands up and turning to Norman, says,

"She's going to dance for us."

As Tanya ducks out of the tent, Norman, looking perplexed, says,
"Who—Tanya?

He stands by watching as the others move the table to one side, arrange six chairs in a half circle facing the flaps. Then Al dimming the lantern, they all sit down, Norman finding himself in the middle, along with Peter.

Gus takes a harmonica from his pocket and begins blowing clean, sweet notes, surprising Norman who did not know Gus could play one. Norman relaxes, waiting for her to prance back in, in her lace bikini underwear—

When lo, she bursts through the flaps—in a black leotard and bare-footed—as Gus, hands cupped around the harmonica, makes it wail.

A Tanya who is no longer Tanya. Only pure movement. Herself the music. As she flows one way—then there. Now trotting with head high. And suddenly poised motionless. Then just as suddenly bounding off...

Norman is amazed by her, by the expressiveness and art of her—that begins to evoke for him the naturalness and beauty and grace of some wild, free forest animal.

When she pauses in front of him, an invisible part of him reaches out to her, touches ever so lightly the heaving breasts.

And now—now that invisible part of him moves past them, beyond those breasts—to an underlying essence that is even more alive than they are.

He seeing her—her—in a way he has never seen anyone before.

When suddenly, from the harmonica, as if from the very bowels of the universe, comes a screeching, shattering, and sustained discord—accompanied by a shrill, human-like scream.

As Tanya crumples into a heap onto the dirt of the floor.

Norman jumps up.

"What the hell is this?"

Just as the light from the lantern goes out—leaving him standing in a pitch-black silence.

An instant later the world explodes back into brightness and form and color, and Norman again sees his Tanya, she now standing before him and balancing on her head and steadying with both hands the magnificent, upright antlers of a bull elk.

What he immediately recognizes as his—Larry's antlers.

The elk-woman goes, "Moooo."

And now Gus is wah-wahing on the harmonica, and voices—Peter's the loudest—are singing,

"Go tell ol' Norman
Go tell ol' Norman
Go tell ol' Norman
His old grey goose is dead."

Harmonica and singing turn into hysterical laughter.

Until finally Norman, as it dawns upon him that these are maybe not such a bad bunch of folks after all—is laughing along with them.

Horses whinny and a mule brays. Which commotion gets Al up from his chair. Looking out through the flaps, he says,

"It's Matt and Marv with the beer and the booze—and just in time too."

15. The Last Sheepeater

Jack, his forehead pressed against the window of the Cessna, and peering down at Tag Creek, speaks into his headset to the pilot beside him.

The tiny plane, roaring steadily, heads straight for a wall of the canyon, and at the last possible moment, banks tightly, and then dropping, makes a low pass over the spot that Jack had indicated, while Jack rotates some dials on the apparatus that sets on his lap.

Again he speaks into the headset.

The plane continuing down the canyon above its shimmering creek begins climbing. And soon emerges into the much larger canyon containing the Salmon River. Below them, Jack can make out the V of a jet boat moving upriver—quickly loses sight of it, as the plane, still gaining elevation, turns for home.

The jet boat, roaring and skimming the green surface of the river, veers towards shore. And its engine dying, now glides— ts prow riding up on and coming to rest on a gravel beach. A dark-skinned man wearing a baseball cap and his black hair hung in a braid hops out onto the sand, letting the large packsack slung over one shoulder slip to the ground.

As the waves of the wake lap the shore, the tanned boatman says,

"Like I said, Curly—the trail up out of this canyon to Goat Point is a real bitch—look up there—when you finally break out on top of those cliffs that seem to kiss the sky—well they don't— that's only halfway—one long-ass haul to photograph a bunch of goats."

"I like to walk uphill—it keeps me strong," says Curly, shoving the prow back into the water.

The two of them wave. And the engine catching, the jet boat swings around, and then, picking up speed, swoops roaring back down river and disappears around a bend.

Curly puts on the pack, crosses the strip of gravel beach, and picks his way through some boulders and currant bushes up to a small grass flat. Where, screwed to the huge reddish trunk of a ponderosa pine, a brown wooden sign points the way to Goat Point. But instead of taking the trail to Goat Point, he turns down river, and is soon among boulders, working his way around the ones he can and clambering over others, the river a stone throw on his right.

Coming to the dense, tangled brush lining a creek that pours down out of a side canyon, he turns uphill onto a thin, almost non-existent elk trail that parallels the creek just above the brush. And placing each foot with care, slowly traverses the steep grassy rock and ponderosa-studded side slope.

A five-foot long rattlesnake winds sliding from under the shade of a mountain mahogany bush and between his legs and down the hillside toward some clumps of sagebrush.

"I am so sorry my brother—to have disturbed you."

The side canyon becoming narrower and rockier, and too steep for further travel, and the elk trail disappearing entirely, he steps, digging in with his heels and half-skidding, downhill and into the brush, where twisting and ducking and pushing away branches, he makes his way to the creek.

Taking off his pack, he leans it against the base of a large cottonwood, golden with fall, and drops onto his belly to drink. He sits against his pack for a while—smelling the brush and fallen leaves and watching the fast-moving water.

"It is very good to be back with all of you who talk to me—always teaching me—in a way I can understand."

He puts the pack back on, and grabbing a pole to steady himself, and still in his sneakers, enters the creek. And heads upstream, alternately plowing through knee-deep stretches of water rushing between boulders and wading through quiet shallow pools, and now and then climbing over the trunk and through the branches of a down cottonwood, Doug fir, or ponderosa.

Eventually, he passes a break in the canyon wall on his right, through which another smaller creek tumbles into the one he is walking up. He leaves the main creek, and pushing and pulling himself up the steep slope and through the tangle of brush and thorn bushes—emerges onto an open flat bench of grass, sagebrush, and ponderosa pines that sits above the junction of the two creeks.

At the base of a series of rock ledges that rise abruptly skyward, he sees the hogan, built in the old, three-forked-poles style, and covered with bark, its blanketed door facing east. Overcome by a sense of the Navajo notion of place-home, and by a profound feeling of gratefulness, he walks slowly that way.

In front of the hogan, and off to one side, a brush-roofed ramada shelters a neat stack of firewood, a fire pit, and a one-foot-high table made from thin poles lashed together with twine, upon which are several carved wooden bowls. From nails driven into the vertical posts of the ramada hang an enamelware kettle, a frying pan, a coffee pot, a ladle carved from mountain sheep horn, and some willow storage baskets.

He stops for a minute to look over a high, thorny brush fence that encloses a garden—from which a black irrigation hose angles uphill and disappears into the alder-choked ravine of the smaller creek.

He goes over to the door of the hogan, slides his pack to the ground, and calls, "Toma."

A woman as dark as himself pushes her way out past the blanket and throws her arms around him.

"As always," she says, "I missed you most at night—and thought wild thoughts."

They stand there laughing and feeling one another.

Until Toma, releasing him, says, "Better tonight—and our two daughters?"

"They say they are doing well in college—and still do not understand why we having been back here since March—for half a year now—you have never come with me when I go for supplies—and instead would rather remain here with your and their Sheepeater-Shoshone ancestors who once lived here."

"And still do—their education—I am afraid—lets them understand less and less—I must pray more often for them."

"They both want to visit us here at Thanksgiving—and so does your mother—and your uncle Charlie and your grandmother too."

"That would be wonderful—then maybe our children will begin to understand."

At the Ranger Station, Jack spreads out his map of the River of No Return Wilderness, and pointing, says to Eliot,

"A couple of times now I've gotten radio signals from this exact same spot by this creek—so the remains of the lion is either lying there—or else it lost its collar there—anyway—I'm thinking of hiking in there."

"With Gail?"

"She's in Boise visiting her folks."

"With all the rock cliffs—I'm not sure you can even get into there—and it's so far down in a canyon that if you did and got hurt you wouldn't have radio communication out—but the heck—what would you say to me coming along?—with it hunting season I've had to deal with lots of stupid stuff—and need a break—some people won't like it—

but since I retire soon—and since they care about me so much that they are just waiting for me to go—let them stew."

"Oh and another thing—that area is crawling with snakes—underground heat seeping up through fissures in the rocks helps create perfect winter dens for them."

"We can take turns going first."

Wolf, wearing only shorts and sandals, and without his backpack, makes his way down the Tag Creek Canyon toward the Salmon River, staying on the steep relatively open side slope above the brush, rose hips, and thimble berries of the canyon bottom. Now and then he speaks to the two wolves ahead of him—a black one and a white one—who have been nuzzling and nudging him this way and that.

Coming to a high, sheer-walled gorge, he heads downhill, and entering the brush, pushes, ducks, and squeezes his way to the creek.

He steps into the water and follows its noisy rush over and around boulders—the two wolves wriggling through the thick brush along one shore. In places he lies down in the water, letting the current take him feet first, and in the deeper pools he ducks his head and swims a few strokes. He passes a small cave. Passes a rattlesnake coiled on a ledge. Some late-blooming, red flowers.

At the top of a waterfall-like chute, he sits down, and sliding—shoots splashing into the largest pool so far.

And standing back up in the chest-deep water, wiping water from his eyes, sees off to one side, a naked, dark-skinned woman standing in a patch of grass watching him.

Wolf feeling their energies mingling, hears her say,

"Let me put my clothes on so that we do not do here in the grass the thing I see you are thinking."

She steps into a pair of jeans.

"So you don't find me too old?—that makes me feel very good."

Then cupping a hand under each breast, she says, raising them slightly,

"They used to point almost straight out—like this."

Laughing, she picks up a T-shirt and pulls it on, and says,

"I see you have learned to talk without words—and about things words cannot speak—like the animals—that is why we connect so well—come with me and meet my husband—we live here."

Curly drags the end of the black irrigation hose from the garden over to the cherry tree he planted several months ago. He opens the nozzle and watches the stream of water flow into the saucer-like depression in which the tree sets.

Looking up, he sees Toma appear out of the brush—and following her, a young half-naked white man, a *belagonna*, but this one radiating sheer aliveness and alertness, and whose each step seems to place him in the exact center of the world he is moving through.

As if guided by the same power that guides the animals—and the sun and the moon and stars.

As Curly looks deeply into the *belagonna* eyes that shine blue into his, Toma says,

"He was a little embarrassed telling me—but he says his name is Wolf—he has been in these mountains almost as long as we have—and I am sure he would like something to eat."

"Wolf—huh—my people—when they were not yet called Navajo—and before they took up sheep herding—danced in wolf skins and sang wolf songs in order to become wolves and thus obtain their power—but now the only ones who become wolves are the witches—those we call skin walkers—but I can tell you are not a witch—so welcome my wolf brother—to what we have here."

Wolf says, "This is a beautiful place—warm and kind—and thank you very much—but I want you to know that I have a supply of dried mushrooms and jerked elk back at my camp—I don't want to take your food."

Toma says, "Wolf—being an Indian is feeding everyone who comes to the door."

"And having alcoholic relatives put the touch on you whenever they see you," says Curly.

Toma and Curly laugh.

Toma says, "I will start a fire—and fix some Navajo blue corn cakes—baked in coals and ashes—and prepare a Shoshone chokecherry-gooseberry sauce for them—or if you wish—you may smear some peanut butter on the cakes."

Curly shuts off the water, saying,

"And afterwards—if you like—why not go back to your camp and gather up your things—and come stay with us?"

That evening in the hogan, the two of them lying on some sheepskins, Curly says,

115

"It seems that for our new brother who will come to live with us—this thing that comes to Indians in dreams—or through ceremonies—or a sacred quest—and dissolves the world that is so often mistaken for the real one—has happened as if by itself."

"Why are you so sure he will come back?"

"Possibly—because he still needs to learn about being with people—and that one does not thrive by acquiring power for oneself— but rather by using it to serve others—and also because—I think he would like to press his body to yours."

"If that should happen—I will tell you—and that it too just happened—as if by itself."

The next afternoon, as Wolf, his pack on his back, starts up the rock ledges behind the hogan to set up his tarp, he says to Toma and Curly,

"I like to see out—and who is coming."

Toma starts a fire. She says to Curly,

"He is a warrior— and knows how to live in a dangerous world."

An hour later, in the shade of the ramada, a clean tablecloth covering the low pole table, the three of them sit down on the ground to a dinner of roasted sheep ribs, potatoes from the garden, and coffee.

Wolf asks Curly where he got the sheep.

Curly tells him on top of a nearby mountain, a bit back from the edge of one of its almost sheer faces, where a circular rock-walled hunting blind still stands that was built very long ago— inside of which he had patiently sat and waited, a pile of sagebrush that he had carried up with him masking his smell.

And when a line of ewes and lambs, followed by a single ram, had come ambling along the edge of the cliff, a route that let them watch the country below them, he had drawn his bow and released an arrow—it missing the ram, who possibly thought it was a passing bird.

He had shot again, the arrow this time penetrating into the ram's chest and partway out the other side.

"My arrows I make from the shoots of willow that grows along the creek, and from blue jay feathers, and the points by pressure flaking the glass of a broken beer bottle."

Curly grabbing another rib, says, "And all that is no shit."

Toma tells Wolf that very long ago her people were desert dwellers in what is now Nevada, who lived mostly on the seeds of plants, along with some rabbits and an occasional antelope, and that about a thousand years ago some of those people wandered north and into these mountains, where displacing others who had lived here for a very long time, they became known as Tukudika—Sheepeaters.

"They were always walkers—a peaceful mountain people—they are still my people—and I have come here to mingle with the dust of their bones—and to feel the presence of the old lives—and to try to see with their eyes—put myself back into a world that some people say goes only forward—but that goes in many directions."

"And now me Wolf—a thousand years later—gnawing on sheep ribs with the last Sheepeater."

It almost dark, Toma and Curly, carrying a pot of rose hip tea and some wooden bowls to drink from, climb up to visit Wolf in his new home. Arriving at his blue tarp, Toma says,

"Look—he has built a rock wall to keep away the wind—and he can see the weather forming—and mountains—and their tops now glowing golden in the last sunlight—that rise up from across the Salmon River—it is very nice here—except that it is missing a woman—and children running about."

Wolf places a plastic bowl of dried mushrooms on the ground and invites them to sit down.

Curly says, "Toma speaks to the point—even the all-mighty Sun who lights up the Navajo world—once said—What good is all I do, if I must survive all my days and nights alone?"

"Not all relationships work out."

Curly pours tea into the wooden bowls, and hands one to Wolf, and one to Toma. And says,

"That is very true—and that is why our Creation story teaches that men and women are equally deserving of respect—and that without harmony between them—there can be no harmony in the universe."

Wolf, sipping his tea, and thinking for the first time in a long while about Cowgirl, about Peggy, says,

"But if two people are as different as night from day?"

"As maybe a Shoshone is from me, a Navajo?—I have found that what appear to be opposites give strength and significance to one another—tell me what is night without day?

Curly goes on, "Many of my Navajo friends do not agree—but I have found that for me—in the world as it now is—many ways of seeing the world is more useful and true than just one."

"Also—that connecting to what is most different from one helps one feel the Oneness of All Things."

Wolf says, "I think I understand."

Toma says, "Sharing a blanket with an Indian woman—you would understand even better."

That night Toma lopes effortlessly alongside her wolf mate through the bright green forest, the two of them out front, leading their pack. They play chase with the raven, urinate at the same spot, couple hard and often—and sleep huddled together in a furry heap.

When Toma wakes up from her wolf sleep, she shakes Curly awake to tell him that it happened—and that the raven blessed them."

"We Navajo have stories that tell of certain special women who mated with the animals—Deer Woman—and Snake Woman—and who then were able to bring back knowledge—and help the people."

"The Shoshone too—I feel I may have a power I did not have before."

Curly, placing a hand on her warm thigh, says, "Show me."

"I am sure we will wake up Wolf," says Toma, putting her hand on his and laughing.

"He I am sure is accustomed to the howling of wolves in the night."

The early morning light filling the canyon, Wolf sits in his sleeping bag watching Toma chop wood down below him. Start the fire. Fill a pail with water from the black hose. And feels a connection to her that he cannot explain. When he sees Curly come out of the hogan, he goes down to join them for breakfast.

The first thing Wolf says is,

"In the middle of the night I woke up in a cave—lying beside an Indian woman—and then I fell asleep again—and dreamed that it was morning and that I was lying alone under my blue tarp.

"And it struck me that what we think of as our normal life is the strangest dream of all."

Mid-morning the three of them go into the garden to pick squash—which they then, making several trips, carry back to the ramada. There, sunlight now streaming into their part of the canyon, they split open the squash, scrape the seeds into a basket, and slice the bright, orange flesh into long spiral strips.

When Wolf comments on the enormous size of the squash, Curly says that is because he and Toma had gathered some grass and other vegetation from along the creek, mixed in some fish heads, the remains of game kills, and some elk and bear shit, made a tea from the mixture, and fed it to the plants.

Toma says, "They are our kin—we pray for them—and talk to them—let them know how much we appreciate the uniqueness and importance of who they are."

"Then we pull them out of the ground—and eat them," says Curly, laughing.

And hangs a bright orange strip on a line hung between the posts of the ramada to dry.

After lunch, Toma rolls up two Navajo blankets, and throwing both over a shoulder, goes down to the big pool to wash them.

Wolf and Curly, taking with them an ax, a machete, and some pieces of rope, hike up a sagebrush-covered hillside. Where searching out the dead branches, they cut and bundle firewood.

Backpack it down to the ramada. And return for more.

As Wolf follows Curly back up the hillside, he becomes aware that—even with Curly walking far ahead of him and Toma down by the pool he cannot see—there exists an almost palpable, physical connection that permeates and cancels the space between him and them.

And realizes that nothing makes one feel better than this—being part of the pack.

"You wolves—you don't know how good you two have it back here—never having known a life in which what people call happiness is an occasional ice cream cone to make up for the loneliness and all the rest of it."

Curly stopping, and turning around, says, "Huh?"

Jack and Eliot, hindered by their heavy packs, slowly pick their way down the precipitous, final stretch of a ridge that falls away into Tag Creek—winding between the ponderosa pines, mountain mahogany, sagebrush, and the numerous rock outcroppings, some of which they down climb, handing down the packs.

Their way blocked by a vertical drop off, they cut down into the drainage to one side of them, holding on to the branches of whatever bushes they can. And eventually bottoming out, come to alders and gurgling water. They follow the flow, fighting their way past the tangle of alders.

Eliot, from up front, says, "What the hell is this?"

And a few moments later both of them find themselves staring at a small pool that has been formed by damming the little creek with rocks and plastic. Lying on the bottom of the pool and held down with rocks is the end of a black hose with a piece of screening wrapped and tied around the inlet—the hose then snaking and angling away from the stream down the mountain.

"Someone is growing marijuana," says Jack, "We could get our heads blown off."

Eliot says, "Let's stash our packs back in the brush and scope it out from above—and then make a plan."

"Sounds good to me."

They go back up the creek a short ways, drop their packs, head up out of the alders. Then work their way back down along the hillside, keeping the hose in sight below them. Coming to a series of rock ledges, they become intent, as carefully moving from foothold to foothold to handhold, they lower themselves.

Jack says, "Look over there—they've got a house and a garden and everything—the only tall stuff I see growing looks like corn."

Eliot says, "What the hell—and two Indian blankets hanging on a clothes line."

Just then they hear a voice from the rock ledge above them say, "Hey—you guys lost?—or what?"

Startled—they look up and see a young man sitting under a blue tarp and looking down on them.

Eliot says, "What's going on here?"

"Some people live here—that's all."

"How long have they been doing that?"

"They say for thousands of years."

"Yeah?—well my name is Eliot and I'm with the Forest Service—and it's my job to inform all of you that all of you are in violation of a couple of laws."

It crosses Wolf's mind that all it would take—would be to roll down some boulders.

When Toma asks Eliot and Jack if they would like a cup of tea, and some smoked salmon, Jack says no thank you, that they have a schedule to meet, having to find a collared mountain lion that is part of an important radio-tracking project and that is probably lying dead down by the creek.

Curly asks how they collared the lion, and Jack says he treed it this past winter with barking hounds, shot a tranquilizer dart into its hip, went up the tree using climbing spurs, and then lowered the cat down hanging by its hind legs on a rope—

Eliot interrupts, saying that what he would like to talk to everyone about is that a federally designated Wilderness such as the one they are in is defined by statute as a place where man shall be a visitor and not remain, and also where nature and its processes are to be left undisturbed and in their natural condition—so that the American people and future generations may enjoy that place forever in all its pristineness.

Curly says, "All of us are brief visitors on this earth—the White Man too will pass."

"The law says you can stay in one spot for only 10 days."

Curly says, "But we are hurting nothing—every day we pray for the plants and the animals—we even pray for the mountains—we help give all of this that is surrounding us life—and so help preserve it forever."

"You put in a water system—and planted a cherry tree."

Toma says, "People do not come to this place—no one will see them."

"I see them—I'm sorry—but these laws have their purpose— like what if the whole Shoshone tribe were to move back here?—and some of the old hippies?—and the Nez Perce who have treaty rights to this area—why before you know it—there would be roads—logged-out clear cuts—and a real estate development and gambling casino at every trail junction—is that what you'd want?—for your children?"

Wolf says, "If these people stayed here—I don't think any of that would happen."

"I have to ask that you leave—take all your things back out with you—and also make everything look as if no one was ever here—I'm sorry—but those are the rules—and this is a nation of law."

Wolf says, "A nation that has broken hundreds of legally binding treaties with the indigenous people of this continent—and that to this day still uses force and deception to dispose of the political leadership of a multitude of small, powerless, sovereign nations—and—"

Toma says, "And if we do not leave?"

"I will give you one week—after that—I would have no choice but to send some peace officers in here to evict you."

"And how will the peace officers do that?—because until the raven tells me otherwise—I cannot leave this place."

"They will have guns."

Toma says, "Are you sure you will not stay for some tea—the fish is very good."

"Thanks again—but we have important work to do—and besides—accepting a dinner would be against the rules too—I hope you understand."

Wolf says, "These people understand everything."

As Eliot and Jack head back for their packs, Wolf says,

"Both of you stayed very calm—and gracious."

Curly says, "I have found that it is always better to just listen— and to watch—they are who they are—and do not really see you or hear you anyway."

And Toma says, "To argue—try to change the other—only arouses ire in both—does one try to change the direction of an icy wind?"

"As soon as I saw those two—even from a distance—I could feel myself getting pissed off."

Curly says, "Once that happened it was too late—and you reentered their world—and like them could no longer see."

He spits on the ground, "What I am talking is not Indian talk— because once I too was a very angry man—but finally and just very recently—in discovering and beginning to walk the Broad Vision Road—I have come to see that the problem is not people like them— or General Custer—who are only acting according to what life has so far taught them and made them into."

Curly looking Wolf right in the eye, says,

"Shoveling them and modern civilization into a sack and dropping it down a deep hole would solve nothing."

"What my husband left out—s that walking the Broad Vision Road—he still sometimes trips on a rock and falls flat on his face."

"Yes—because it is a very difficult Road—and also because to see—sometimes falling on one's face is very necessary," says Curly, laughing.

Wolf, lying in the shade of his tarp, his eyes closed, goes over in his mind how much of his life has been spent in crazy, futile opposition to the way things and especially other people are.

It occurs to him that Curly's Broad Vision Road could also be called the Compassion Road—and that there is no one who does not know suffering, that there is no one who has it all exactly right.

He sits up with a start.

"Why hello, wolves—so here you two are again—I now see that as soon as our visitors appeared I again got caught up in stuff—and forgot about you."

"Is that why you ran off?"

A raven flies crawking over the hogan. Curly and Toma step outside, and looking up, watch as it circles once, now crawking even more, and then continues down the canyon—flapping and getting smaller.

Curly says, "Do you suppose it is going to the lion?"

"Maybe that too—however as she passed over—she told me that I may now leave these mountains whenever I choose to—but that since I am descended from the small handful of Tukudika that did not surrender to the American army—under no circumstances should I permit anyone to run me out—and then she wished me well—and said good-by."

She pauses, and continues.

"We have a juniper bow and some arrows and an axe—and a machete—and could possibly send Wolf off to bring in a television crew—but eventually—we would still be run out."

"About a half mile upstream from the big pool is a large cave—its entrance hidden by brush—that was used not only by the Tukudikabut by those who lived here before them and who chipped beautiful pictures into the walls of the rock—that speak of the World That Lies On the Other Side of This One."

"Huh—so your idea is that we should—like disappear—into the Other World."

"I think we should move our things—our wood and food up there—and when the peace officers come with their guns—hide out there—and make no fire or noise—until they are gone."

"And the hogan and the garden?—and the cherry tree?"

"Leave them as they are—it would be nice to move back again—when everyone is gone—they may be too lazy to destroy them."

"The cave is the special place you have been going to after you bathe?"

"Yes—to just sit in its coolness—listening to the rush of the creek—whose sound often turns into beautiful songs more beautiful than

123

any I have heard before—and sometimes the long spear point asleep in a corner wakes up and speaks to me—and I hear the shouts of playing children—and once heard the grunts of an animal much larger than any elk or bear—and twice the same raven that just passed overhead has flown by—blessing me."

"It is wonderful that your raven friend has led you back to yourself—and to the wolves that were once so abundant—and to your Tukudika ancestors—and to the people before them who thrust spears into animals much larger than elk or bear."

"Through you—your medicine—your gift—others will come to see that the world is not as they had thought it was—and glimpsing its true essence—be healed."

"When I was a still a girl my grandmother told me that refusing such a gift—and choosing something else—one falls very sick—and will then die without a light in one's eyes."

Eliot stares for a while at the rattlesnake, its head resting across its coils, there in the shade of his pack.

He picks up a stick, and tries to nudge it away.

The snake, its rattle now buzzing, raises and winds the upper half of its body into the air in an S, its long forked tongue thrust out and erect. Eliot steps quickly back—

Just as it lunges dart-like toward his hand. Dropping his stick, he steps stumbling backwards into some brush—trips, and regains his balance.

Feels something slam painfully into the back of his lower left calf, and twisting frantically around, sees the second snake as it retreats sliding off and disappears in some rocks.

"Damn it," he yells.

And again he yells, this time louder, "Damn it."

Jack arriving and seeing Eliot sitting on the ground pulling up a pant leg, says,

"What's up?"

"A snake got me—and it hurts like hell—Jesus—look at these two fang punctures."

"Yeah—it got you all right—lie down on your back—and I know it's not easy—but try to relax—you don't want to circulate more venom than you have to—breathe slow and deep—slow and deep— that's it— let me get you your sleeping bag to prop your head up on."

"It was a very big one Jack."

"With those at the hogan—there are four of us—we'll try to get you down to the river—and flag down the first tourist raft or jet boat that comes by."

"What if one doesn't?—or it doesn't stop?—Jesus—what a drag."

"Don't move—and stay calm—stay calm—you'll be OK—I'm going to get the others," says Jack, starting down the hill.

Eliot calls out to Jack and to the forest, "It's going to be dark soon."

Ten minutes later, Jack, Wolf, Curly and Toma arrive running.

Jack says, "How are you feeling?"

"Woozy—it really hurts—and scared."

Curly says, "In this grass and brush—close to the coolness of this quiet little creek—is a wonderful place for snakes to rest in the afternoon."

As Toma, kneeling down, lays both hands gently on the swollen calf, one on either side of the punctures, Eliot immediately feels a slight tingle, and then a soothing warmth entering the leg, and also him.

"My people have much experience curing these bites—I will help you—but not only must you let me—but also trust and believe in me."

Staring up at the dark, oddly-beautiful woman, whose hands still rest on him, and who has a brilliant light in her eyes, Eliot says,

"Yes—anything—please go ahead."

"Good—then first I will try to suck out what I can of the poison—and perhaps some other harmful things—and your job is to receive that which will come to assist us—so you must let yourself open up—and when you feel it trying to enter—let it flow into and occupy all of you—not just the leg."

"What you described—may already be happening."

"That is a very good sign—my husband will help me—you must have faith in him too."

Toma bends over, grips the leg firmly, and putting her mouth over both punctures, sucks forcefully and long, now and then producing a slurping sound—and then spits on the ground beside her. And sucks again, as Curly, now kneeling across from her, begins chanting in what might be Navajo.

Eliot can feel the strange, insistent syllables drumming in every cell of his body, and their force slowly repositioning him, placing him, Eliot, in the center of a very special—a very warm and sacred universe, in which he too feels very special and sacred.

He becomes aware that these two people seem to be seeing things that are very far away and that he cannot. And tries to be with them, and to see too.

The sucking, and then the chanting stop. He closes his eyes.

He feels the light touch of hands that he knows are Toma's on his head. Then—as sounds like none he has ever heard begin to involuntarily escape from her throat, letting out the song being sung inside her, from maybe very far back in time—he feels the fingertips running in soft, brushing strokes down his body, the song, incredibly eerie and beautiful, now flowing powerfully like an unending river through him, as the fingers, or whatever they are, continue their brushing, now down along his arms, now down his legs.

And he surrenders totally to the first real peace he has ever known, and uttering a choking sob, sinks into an unconsciousness—in which the song, and the caresses, go on and on and on.

Almost dark—Toma asks Jack and Wolf to help Curly haul mud from along the creek.

When Eliot opens his eyes, he sees an Indian woman sitting beside him, lit by the glow of a fire. He becomes aware that he is lying on a blanket, with another one draped over him, and of something heavy and cool pressing against his hurt leg. Trying to move the leg, he cannot.

"Where am I—what happened to my leg?"

"You are not far from where the snake bit you—your leg is buried in a pile of mud—and there are some small logs holding everything in place—and soon you will be better—the others are sleeping nearby."

Looking at her shimmering in the firelight, Eliot believing totally—falls peacefully back into sleep.

When Eliot wakes up, the sun is already poking above the high canyon wall, its light filtering down through the branches of the few pines around him. He is immediately aware that he feels better and that his leg no longer hurts as much. He sees Toma and Jack sitting by the fire.

He sits up, and looking at his lower leg, buried under the pile of mud, hears Jack say,

"Good morning—how's it going?"

"Much better."

Jack comes over to him, followed by Toma, carrying a coffee pot.

"Jack and I will dig out your leg—and clean you up."

126

They pull the logs and the mud away from the leg. Then Toma slowly pours warm water from the coffee pot on the leg and wipes with her other hand, cleaning it.

"Although there is still some discoloration—the swelling is down—you will be well very soon—so please try to stand up—Jack and I will help you down to the ramada—where it will be easier to take care of you."

Eliot standing up, beams Toma a big smile. She smiles back.

"There's still some mud on your leg."

As she walks with the coffee pot over to the creek, Eliot, watching the rocking of the round, woman hips, realizes he is already almost as good as new.

Wolf coming back from a lope with the two wolves, finds Toma at the ramada, stirring a pot banked with coals from the fire.

"I am boiling a tasty breakfast gruel for us and our visitors—of ground squash seeds."

"I saw Eliot is limping—but about—it looks like you've cured him."

"Who ever knows these things?—perhaps the snake did not inject much venom—having not been very angry—or having bitten a pack rat or some other creature a short while before."

The white glow of the moon shows from behind a cloud, as Eliot and Jack arrange their sleeping bags under one end of the ramada.

"You know Jack—it's not so much them maybe saving my life the way they did that has me confused—but feeling more warmth and caring than I ever have before—and also something else I can't seem to put my finger on—it's almost like—and that's exactly itI don't know what it's almost like."

"I know what you mean—I won't be able to quite explain this to anyone either."

"Like here they are—still looking after and feeding the bastard who is evicting them—anyway I don't feel right—being here—and I wonder if maybe—even though my leg still hurts some—we should just push on down to the Salmon—and catch a raft or jet boat out of here."

"I think we should split too—leave the lion to the coyotes, ravens, and bears—somehow radio tracking them—now and then dissecting one—recording a bunch of numbers—doesn't seem to be the most important thing in the world anymore—I want to get back to Gail—

she'll be getting back tomorrow—you can't imagine how much I miss her—and that's only part of what I'm feeling—and need to think about."

Eliot says, "I'll leave them my brand new hunting knife—and stick some bills inside the sheathe."

The next morning, which is overcast, and it having just started to drizzle, Wolf, dressed in sandals and shorts, and carrying Eliot's pack, steps into Tag Creek—followed by Jack in his poncho, and then Eliot in his, a chest-high pole in each hand bracing him.

The three of them heading downstream, Wolf turning his head, says,

"Let us know if you want us to take turns piggy backing you—we can always stash the packs and Jack and I can come back for them once we get you to the river."

"So far it's going good—but let's watch for snakes—Curly told me there's a den down this way—and that they can swim."

It still drizzling, the clouds lowering, and a wall of fog rolling down Tag Creek—Eliot and Jack pick up some pieces of driftwood from a white sand beach and carry them up to the somewhat drier ground at the base of a large Doug fir.

While Jack clears away a circle of duff and then arranges some sticks in the form of a tepee for the fire—Eliot stands there, under the tree, watching the quiet, smooth glide of the wide, green river, the River of No Return.

"You know Jack—I feel like we somehow just slid down out of a long tunnel—to a place where the last couple of days never really happened—so maybe that's the way we should leave it—as a dream."

"I don't get you—from up on the ridge we dropped into Tag Creek—couldn't find the lion—you tripped and botched your leg on some branch stubs—and now here we are—trying to flag down a raft or a jet boat—of course it happened."

Eliot glances at Jack's stick tepee.

"Those pieces look pretty damp—I'll whittle some dry shavings."

He goes to his pack, rummages in it, and says,

"Darn it Jack—I think I lost my new hunting knife."

"Darn it."

Toma, Curly, and Wolf move their few things, firewood, and food to the cave.

128

Move there themselves—and wait for the men with the guns.
The day they should have come passes.

On a warm, Indian summer afternoon, the three of them bathing
and splashing in the deep pool, Curly says,
"Maybe what happened—is that Toma's medicine has changed
the way the world usually works."
Toma ducks underwater, and emerging, says,
"Or maybe with the three of us coming together as we have—our
power is now such that that is what has changed the way the world
usually works."

Another week goes by. And another.
They move back to the hogan—to the garden and the cherry tree.
One morning, as Wolf goes over to the garden to pull up a
cabbage, the two wolves jump up on him. Then unexpectedly leave him
to run up the ridge a ways—and returning, jump up on him again, this
time almost knocking him down.
That evening, Wolf sitting with Curly and Toma around the
glowing embers of the campfire, shares with them a story of two
wolves—a white one and a black one.
Toma places some sticks on the fire. Then says, very quietly,
"Walking with the spirits of the wolves—or with the spirits of the
big trees—or with the spirits of the ancient ones who once lived here—
or with Jesus—holding such things in one's heart—helps one stay aware
at every moment of which aspects of what one encounters in the world
are inventions and fantasies of the human brain—and which are real."
As the sticks flare up, Curly says, "Should you find that you
become very good at walking in the two worlds at the same time—you
may find you no longer need the wolves—and may want to send them
away—since it will be very hard for them out there in the place you will
eventually have to go back to."
When Wolf describes how just this morning the wolves had
jumped up on him to let him know the time has come for him to return
to Peggy, Toma says,
"That is wonderful—but expect nothing—because a woman—
once she has offered all of herself to a man who for whatever good
reason is at that moment not ready for her—may find herself never able
to offer him that gift again."

Curly says, "Some flowers when they bloom—stay open longer than others."

The next morning, as Wolf, his pack on his back, starts up the ridge out of Tag Creek, Curly shouts,
"We will be looking for you at Thanksgiving."
And Toma shouts, "Ask Peggy for a calendar—to make sure you get the day right."
And then pointing, says softly to Curly,
"Do you see what I see?"
"A sagebrush-covered hillside?"
"No—the two wolves—that Wolf has just said good-bye to—cutting up through the sagebrush to join up with and play with the raven."

16. Into the Clouds

By cold November, up in the high country, the elk have migrated down into the warmer Salmon River Breaks—to winter there.

This morning, up in the high country, a weasel runs along the top poles of an empty corral, dislodging clumps of new snow—as Larry, leading two heavy-packed mules, rides away from his boarded-up log cabin and across Wapiti Meadow.

Breaking trail through the snow, crashing through the iced-up creek—they are soon winding among the snow-laden lodgepole pines.

Out to the Ranger Station and road's end—before the land is irrevocably snowed in.

Feeling a weariness and peacefulness, almost a warmth in his bones, Larry relaxes, sits back in the saddle, he content to be done with another season of working trail, content to let the winter storms do what they will with this wilderness.

A wilderness too—finally at peace.

The season that he lived so intensely already seems—just as all the others before them—like a stone that went ker-plunk. Leaving only ripples which are no longer the stone.

By noon, a thick white fog having blown in, and the day no warmer, he stops to reposition the packs on Sergeant and to tighten cinches. And is off again, clip clop, clip clop, munching a tuna sandwich.

Bits of Anne's unexpected and surprisingly long letter roll around in his mind.

I feel very changed....

I continue to want to stand by those we sometimes call the underclass—and so continue wanting to work in legal services. Even though I now see more clearly than before that one cannot really look to the legal system for the fairness and justice and the compassion that the world so urgently needs.

Just as one cannot look to an educational system for learning how to live well. Nor to any church to connect one to what some have labeled with the word God, but that is so much more than any word or words can suggest.

I can only look to myself for those things, and make it my priority to walk well in the world—come whatever hell or efforts of others to dissuade me...

131

And I have recently learned that to walk well I will need to keep one foot in wilderness, in what is forever wild—to sort of repeat Thoreau. In that which in some way may still be our essence...

When you come out of the woods in the fall, and should you take a hankering, come visit me here in East St. Louis. There are no mountains. But Monk's Mound, which as I may have already told you is the largest man-made earth mound in North America, is just across the river. To remind us that civilizations, the worlds we put together, are much more fragile than are elk and bear grass...

It beginning to snow again, Larry hunches his shoulders against the rough weather that toughens a man and is no enemy.

A roaring jet boat skimming the green surface of the river that is sometimes called the River of No Return, heads toward shore. Its engine dying, it glides into a shallow eddy near the mouth of Tag Creek— where Curly hops out into the knee-deep water and guides the prow onto the gravel shore.

A young woman, Tingu, his daughter, giving him her hand, hops out onto the gravel, then Sally, his other daughter, and then Pona, their grandmother, a brightly-colored, striped blanket wrapped around her.

Pona's brother, Charlie, hands Curly an enormous pack sack, and another one, and then one after another the plastic mesh shopping bags filled with groceries. From the rear of the boat, an ancient wrinkled woman, Habitse, also wrapped in a colorful blanket, works her way to the prow, followed closely by the boatman.

When Curly, Charlie, and the boatman all simultaneously move to help her out, she waves them away, saying,

"I will do this myself—to show you I am still tough son of bitch."

And climbs out onto the gravel.

The boatman says to Charlie, "How old is she?"

Charlie climbing out, says, "The mother of an old man like me— has to be enough up in years—that she is ageless and holy."

Curly and Charlie push the boat back into deep water. Everyone waves. The boatman positions himself behind the steering wheel. And the engine catching, the boat swings around, and then picking up speed, swoops roaring downriver.

Hearing a shout, they all turn around and see Toma running down across the rock-strewn gravel beach toward them.

Behind her, ambling along and holding hands, come a white man and a white woman, she wearing roper boots and a cowgirl hat.

And behind those two the canyon wall rises abruptly—its upper portion under snow—up into the clouds.

About the Author

Rolf Goerke worked for some 20 seasons out of a Forest Service cabin located 30 miles from the nearest road, in the heart of Idaho's River of No Return Wilderness. In the off-seasons, he worked as an Outward Bound Instructor in Big Bend National Park and in the back country of Mexico.

He is married to a Tarahumara and presently lives part of the year with her and their young son among her people on the rim of Mexico's Copper Canyon-- again, far from the nearest road. The rest of the year, he and his family live in a small cabin beside the Tularosa River in New Mexico.

His other published novel, *The Least Among Them*, about a Tarahumara goatherd, contains what is possibly the most comprehensive description of the contemporary Tarahumara Baja culture available.

His novels portray the triumph of the old human center that was rooted in community and in nature over the disarray and dissolution of the human psyche as it finds itself immersed in an increasingly complex, technological, and controlled society.

What he enjoys most is running up and down mountains, and down into and up out of canyons.